Central High School Library

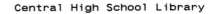

14990   W9-DCV-898

Aleecia

Central High School Library Media Center
116 Rebel Drive
Park Hills, MO 63601

DISCARDED

NINE MONTHS

Aleecia

by Maggie Wells

E

EPIC
Press

Aleecia
Nine Months: Book #2

Written by Maggie Wells

Copyright © 2016 by Abdo Consulting Group, Inc.

Published by EPIC Press™
PO Box 398166
Minneapolis, MN 55439

All rights reserved.

Printed in the United States of America.

International copyrights reserved in all countries.
No part of this book may be reproduced in any form without
written permission from the publisher. EPIC Press™ is trademark
and logo of Abdo Consulting Group, Inc.

Cover design by Candice Keimig
Images for cover art obtained from iStockPhoto.com
Edited by Lisa Owens

LIBRARY OF CONGRESS CATALOGING-IN-PUBLICATION DATA

Wells, Maggie.
Aleecia / Maggie Wells.
p. cm. — (Nine months; #2)
Summary: Fifteen-year-old Aleecia can't believe it when Kyle, the 18-year-old
captain of the football team, falls for her. When she gets pregnant, she tells Kyle, and
he stands by her—at least for a while. Will their love weather Kyle's move to college
while Aleecia waits for him at home in Fort Pierce, Florida? Is he the stand-up guy
she thought he was?
ISBN 978-1-68076-191-7 (hardcover)
1. Teenagers—Sexual behavior—Fiction. 2. Teenage pregnancy—Fiction.
3. High schools—Fiction. 4. Sex—Fiction. 5. Young adult fiction. I. Title.
[Fic]—dc23
2015949411

EPICPRESS.COM

To Jett and Dylan, who taught me everything I know about pregnancy, childbirth and single motherhood

One
ALEECIA

ON A TUESDAY AFTER SCHOOL IN MAY, ALEECIA LOCKED her cherry-red Rally five-speed to the bike rack by the rear employee entrance to Big Lots.

She found the bike on Craigslist by searching for the keywords "Curb Alert." The owner had dumped it in front of his house and she dashed out as soon as she saw the posting, running more than half a mile, hoping to find it still there. The paint on the frame was chipped, the handlebar grips were worn and the derailleur was so rusty that the bike would not stay in gear as she pedaled. But she promised herself that if she ever scraped together enough money, she would take to it a bike shop and have it repaired.

Aleecia scored a lot of free stuff on Craigslist. She found a bookcase for her bedroom, a set of snow tires, and lots of sports equipment: a tennis racket, a bowling ball, and even a basketball hoop.

"Why do you keep dragging this junk home?" her mother groused on a daily basis. "The garage is full to the rafters. What are you planning to do with all this? And what's with snow tires? What do we need snow tires for in Fort Pierce, Florida?"

Aleecia found the allure of free stuff irresistible. Okay, so maybe she wouldn't ever use the bowling ball or the basketball hoop. But the bike was different. The bike gave her freedom. Aleecia rode fast, celebrating the wind in her hair, the burn in her thighs, and the pounding in her chest. She never felt more alive than when she was riding her bike. *After all*, Aleecia thought, *the bike was the reason I got the job at Big Lots. The nice HR lady asked me if I had my own mode of transportation.*

"Mode?" Aleecia asked.

"Do you drive?" the nice lady asked.

"I'm fifteen," Aleecia said.

"Of course," the nice lady said. "Do you have a bike? A motor scooter?"

Aleecia smiled with pride. "Yes," she said. "I have a bike."

//

Aleecia punched in the four-digit code on the security pad outside the employee entrance and grabbed the metal handle, yanking the door with all of her strength. The door swung open with a metallic screech of protest. The back hall was deserted, so she punched her time card before walking to the locker room to store her backpack and change into her Big Lots shirt.

She reported for duty at the manager's office.

"Hey, Mr. Martin," she said. Mr. Martin was a tall, heavy-set man in his thirties.

"Aleecia," he said. "Here is your cash drawer. I need you to relieve Brenda on line nine. Let's go."

Mr. Martin escorted Aleecia to the checkout line and stood back, observing while Brenda logged out and Aleecia logged in.

"I need you to work until closing tonight, Aleecia," Mr. Martin said.

"But, it's a school night, Mr. Martin," Aleecia said. "I'm not supposed to work past eight o'clock on school nights."

"I'm sorry but we're short on clerks tonight," Mr. Martin said. "Marlene got beat up by her boyfriend. You can check out the video on YouTube. Can you believe that? YouTube?" He chuckled. Then his voice turned grave. "Yeah, so I am going to need you to work until closing time until further notice—until we hire a new girl or Marlene gets out of the hospital or something."

Mr. Martin escorted Brenda back to the office,

where she would stand at attention while he counted every dollar and matched it to the register printout.

I am good at checkout, Aleecia thought. Impatient shoppers aggressively maneuvered their overflowing baskets between lanes, seeking the fastest-moving line. The beeps and boops of Aleecia's scanner formed the rhythm of her day and telegraphed to everyone in line how much faster she was than the other checkout girls. She enjoyed the competition and prided herself on her accuracy. *Having to scan an item a second or third time—well, that's just plain amateur!* Aleecia thought. At the end of each shift, the girl with the biggest drawer and the most receipts received a five-dollar bonus. Aleecia went home most days with a crisp five-dollar bill tucked into the pocket of her cut-off shorts.

Store traffic slowed after eight p.m., so Aleecia pulled out her science book and hid it under the conveyor belt to steal peeks when nobody was looking. She was head-down, immersed in memorizing the periodic table when she heard a deep voice.

"Yo."

Aleecia startled and knocked her chemistry book to the floor. Kyle was a senior at Westwood High and captain of the football team. He was at least six-foot-four with ebony skin, a devastating smile, and enormous bedroom eyes.

"You dropped something," Kyle said.

"Whoops." Aleecia quickly bent down to retrieve the book and bumped her head on the conveyor belt.

"I'm sorry," Aleecia said. She stood up; her face flushed. She hurriedly started to scan his items.

"Aleecia, right?" Kyle said.

Aleecia froze; she held a bottle of Batman shampoo in her hand. *He knows my name!* she thought. *The captain of the football team knows my name?*

"That's for my little brother," Kyle said.

Flustered, Aleecia scanned the item and grabbed another.

"I didn't want you to think that I'm into superheroes," Kyle said. "Not any more, anyway."

Aleecia giggled and looked at him. An enormous grin spread across his face and his teeth were dazzling white. She felt her heart fall out of her chest, landing somewhere in the middle of her gut.

"Great season," Aleecia said. She continued to scan his items, but the rhythm of beeps and boops slowed. She wanted the conversation to last.

"You follow football?" Kyle asked.

"Well, I couldn't go to all the games this season, obviously." Aleecia sheepishly gestured toward the cash register. "But the game against Central High—I could not miss that. Even if I had to call in sick that day."

Finally, Kyle's basket was empty. Aleecia told him to swipe his card while she bagged his items and placed them in his cart.

She batted her eyes at him as she waited for the receipt to print. Then she held onto one end of the register slip as he took the other and they locked eyes. *Flirting!* she thought. *I am flirting! And he is flirting back! No one has ever flirted with me before!*

"Hey," Kyle said. "Are you going to the barbecue on Sunday?"

"What barbecue?" Aleecia said.

"It's the end-of-season celebration. It's at State Park Beach at four o'clock," Kyle said. "Are you working on Sunday?"

"No, I'm off on Sunday," Aleecia said. "Sure, I'd love to go. I'll see you there?"

"Okay then," Kyle said as wheeled his cart toward the exit.

Aleecia stood and watched him walk away; his gait was graceful, yet forceful. He walked as a lion would, confident in his dominance. *He asked me out!* she thought. *Is this a date? My first date?*

Aleecia floated through the hours to closing, greeting each customer with a beatific smile and scanning items with superhuman speed. Finally, the announcement came over the loudspeaker: "Attention shoppers, the store is closing in ten minutes."

Mr. Martin escorted Aleecia to his office and counted her out.

"Long day?" he asked. "Don't forget. I need you to close again tomorrow."

"Sure, Mr. Martin," Aleecia said. "Did I make bonus today?"

"When you work a long shift, you're not eligible for bonus," he said.

Aleecia didn't even care. She felt like she was floating on air as she unlocked her bike and pedaled home fast, through the night air thick with the buzzing of insects.

Two

KYLE

O<small>N</small> T<small>UESDAY MORNING</small>, K<small>YLE</small> <small>WOKE TO THE SOUND OF</small> the baby wailing and the smell of stale urine. He groaned and, hopping down from the top bunk, poked at his eight-year-old brother, Dwayne, who was curled up at the foot of his mattress.

"Hey, buddy," Kyle said. "You wet the bed again. Come on, let's get you into the tub."

Dwayne whimpered and rubbed his eyes as Kyle led him into the bathroom and turned on the water.

"Don't tell Mama," Dwayne said.

"Give me your pj's and jump in the tub. I'll put

everything in the washer," Kyle said. "She won't find out."

Kyle poked his head into his mother's room. He was relieved to see that she was home, passed out on the bed within a few feet of the crib where Crystal was bouncing up and down on her toes and rattling the rails of her crib. When Crystal saw him, she quieted down. He glanced again at his mother. *I never know if I'll find the bitch here*, he thought. She had a tendency to disappear for days on end, leaving Kyle to manage the household. He had to feed and bathe his little brother and sister, and drop them off at daycare and school in the morning. Sometimes, when she had been gone for a stretch and he worried that the kids thought they might never see her again, Kyle would put on his mother's robe and pull the little ones close to him so they could smell her scent and pretend that she was there.

His mother didn't even stir as Kyle tiptoed over to the crib and lifted Crystal out.

Back in the kitchen, he changed Crystal's diaper and set her down in her playpen. While he warmed a bottle of formula in the microwave, he gathered all of the soiled sheets and clothes from the bedroom and stuffed everything into the washer. The detergent bottle felt light. He peered inside and made a mental note to add laundry detergent to the shopping list.

The microwave timer rang and he tested the temperature of the formula on his tongue. Crystal took the bottle and sucked at it eagerly, tracking Kyle's movements with her eyes.

Dwayne padded into the kitchen in bare feet, wearing jeans and a Spiderman T-shirt.

"Watch the baby while I get dressed," Kyle said, handing Dwayne a bottle of apple juice and a Pop-Tart, fresh out of the toaster. "Be careful, it's hot."

///

Kyle dropped the baby at his Aunt Georgia's, and Dwayne at Fairlawn Elementary before driving to Westwood High. The bell rang just as he pulled into the parking lot. He glowered into his reflection in the rear-view mirror. *Late again*, he thought.

Kyle walked straight to the assistant principal's office and joined the line of kids in the hallway. Kyle was a regular in Mrs. Johnson's office, as he was often late to school. She knew all about his mom and the situation at home. And being captain of the football team afforded him a certain amount of leeway.

When his turn came, he stepped up to the counter.

"What's it today, Kyle?" asked Mrs. Johnson.

"I had to take care of the kids," Kyle said.

"Your mother went AWOL again?" Mrs. Johnson asked. "Do I need to call Social Services?"

The last time Social Services got involved they had taken Dwayne and Crystal away for a month. Dwayne had been wetting the bed every night since he had returned from the foster home. "No, she is at home," Kyle said. "She just didn't get up this morning."

Mrs. Johnson gave him a sympathetic smile and handed him the late pass.

//

On the way home from football practice, Kyle stopped by Big Lots. He browsed the aisles and loaded his cart with household supplies: detergent, toothpaste, shampoo, tampons (the bitch was always out of tampons), diapers, baby formula, Pop-Tarts, cereal, milk, and cans of pasta. He had managed to select the shopping cart with a bad front left wheel. The cart seemed to have a mind of its own and kept crashing into displays and making a scene.

He eyed the crowd at checkout and saw that line nine was open. He wrestled with his cart, trying to look as nonchalant as possible. As he reached the belt, he saw Aleecia studying something in what looked like a textbook. Every year, the incoming freshman class was scrutinized for hot girls and seniors got first pick. Kyle had noticed Aleecia right away and he had even thought about asking her out, but he was dating Janelle at the time. *I'm just realizing—I haven't seen her in a while*, he thought. *She must work a lot.*

She probably has no idea who I am. He took his time looking her up and down since she was absorbed in her book. He liked the way her breasts strained at her shirt, threatening to burst the top button. She had smooth, pale skin and long, dark, wavy hair.

"Yo," Kyle said.

She looked up at him, startled. Her mouth was open, her lips were ample. He imagined what they would feel like against his. Then her book went crashing to the floor.

"You dropped something," Kyle said.

"Whoops." Aleecia bent down to pick up the book and Kyle felt bad. She seemed flustered as she started to scan the items on the belt.

"I'm sorry," he said. "Aleecia, right?"

Aleecia stood there staring at him and holding a tube of Batman shampoo. Kyle was mortified, embarrassed to be shopping for diapers, tampons for his mom, and little-kid shampoo. What must she be thinking?

"That's for my little brother," Kyle said.

Aleecia didn't seem to think anything of it. She continued scanning his items.

He saw an opening. "I didn't want you to think that I'm into superheroes," Kyle said. "Not any more, anyway."

Then she laughed and looked at him full on. Her tawny eyes sparkled and he turned on the pearly whites. *I've got her; she's in my force field, now*, he thought.

"Great season," Aleecia said.

So she does know who I am? Kyle thought. *The girl is no fool!* "You follow football?" Kyle asked.

"I don't get to the games often." Aleecia gestured toward the cash register. "But the game against Central High—that was awesome!"

Finally his basket was empty. Aleecia said, "Swipe your card."

Kyle held his breath as he swiped his debit card, hoping it would be approved. He had his state-issued SNAP card tucked into his wallet, but he didn't want to use food stamps in front of Aleecia. Growing up in Ft. Pierce was about keeping secrets and passing for normal, pretending everything was fine. He exhaled when the keypad said *approved.*

Aleecia handed him the receipt but she wouldn't let go. *She's a tiger*, he thought. And then he remembered the barbecue on Sunday.

"Are you going?" Kyle asked. "State Park beach at four."

She said something about having to work.

"Too bad," Kyle said. He felt self-conscious as he shoved his cart toward the exit, the front wheel squeaking and dragging and clicking.

That was awkward, he thought. *But, now I know where she works. Yeah, baby, I'll be back!*

Three

ALEECIA

ON SUNDAY MORNING, ALEECIA WOKE UP BEFORE THE alarm went off; she was excited about seeing Kyle. She fixed her hair and dressed for church.

"Bye, Mom," Aleecia yelled as she hopped on her bike. Her mom was dressed in her home aide uniform and waved wearily, a cup of coffee in her hand.

Church was a huge part of Aleecia's life. She sang in the choir, participated in all of the pageants, and volunteered with the youth group. She loved everything about church, the scent of incense, the whispered chants, and then there was the whole ritual of choir—meeting in the rehearsal room at ten fifteen, donning the heavy robe over her cut-off shorts, running through the warm-up, and then the organ accompanying their procession to the choir loft. She felt part of something bigger than herself. The music made her heart soar and sometimes even made her cry. She hung on every word the Pastor spoke and often daydreamed about becoming a minister herself. *That is, if Gospel singing doesn't work out for me*, she thought.

But on this day, she felt a special sense of anticipation. Her cousin Gina had offered to lend her a dress to wear to the barbecue. And her friend Dawn, who had her driver's license, was coming to pick her up at four.

Aleecia found Gina at coffee hour after the service.

"Can we go?" asked Aleecia.

"Excited much?" Gina asked. "You can't let this boy know. You need to play it cool."

"I know, I know," Aleecia asked. "Can we go?" She tugged at Gina's arm.

At Gina's house, Aleecia raced to the closet. "What do you think will look good on me?" she asked.

"With that tight little body, baby, it will all look good on you," Gina said, laughing.

Gina pawed through her closet and pulled out a pink halter dress. "I've never worn this. Let's try it," she said.

Aleecia stripped down to her panties and slipped the dress over her head. It felt tight around her waist.

"Is it too tight?" she asked. She stood in front of the mirror; her nipples were silhouetted by the soft fabric.

"Oh no," Gina said. "You are rocking that dress. Let me fix your face."

Gina pulled out her makeup bag. "Close your eyes," she said.

Gina applied eyeliner and shadow.

"That's too much," Aleecia said.

"No, wait," Gina said. She applied a few more brushstrokes. "Now, look."

Aleecia opened her eyes and looked in the mirror. She grimaced.

"Don't make a face," Gina said, laughing. "Strike a pose. Like Rihanna."

Aleecia struck a pose that she imagined was sophisticated.

Gina laughed. "This boy doesn't stand a chance," she said. "Go easy on him."

//

At four o'clock, Aleecia texted Dawn. Where r u?

Dawn replied. Be there in 2

Dawn pulled into the driveway in a rusted-out pickup. Joyce was riding shotgun.

"Where am I supposed to sit?" Aleecia asked.

"Sit on my lap," Joyce said. "Come on, we can fit."

//

Dawn pulled into the beach parking lot and killed the engine.

"Shit, this place is packed," Joyce said. "This is one *big* party."

Aleecia started to get nervous. Everyone was wearing bikini tops and cut-off shorts. Was she overdressed?

The girls walked out toward the beach. Dawn saw someone she knew and peeled off. Joyce followed. Aleecia stood in the middle of the grassy lawn, wondering what to do.

"Yo," Kyle said.

Aleecia spun around at the sound of his voice.

"I thought you had to work today," Kyle said.

"No," Aleecia said. "I specifically said . . . "

"Hey," Kyle interrupted her. "Do you want something to drink?"

"Okay?" Aleecia said, uncertain.

Kyle took her hand and led her toward a crowd of people who were milling around a picnic table that was littered with beer cans and plastic cups.

"Hey, T.J.!" Kyle called out. "Get me a bottle out of the cooler."

Kyle twisted the top off of a frosty bottle and offered it to Aleecia.

"What is it?" she said.

"Taste it and see if you like it," Kyle said.

Aleecia took a sip. It tasted sweet. She took another sip. "It's good," she said.

"You look nice," Kyle said.

"Do you like my dress?" Aleecia asked.

"That dress was made for you," Kyle said as he slipped his arm around her waist.

Aleecia was surprised at how much she enjoyed the sensation. Her heart exploded like a swarm of plovers over the pounding surf. He was holding her tight and she felt very small next to him, excited, but also scared. Kyle leaned his face down close and Aleecia put her hands on his shoulders, pushing him away.

"There are people watching us," she said.

"Let's go to my car," Kyle said. She felt the eyes of the crowd on her as he took her hand and led her toward the parking lot. She banked every jealous look, her self-worth growing with each one. He opened the passenger door for her and then walked around to the driver's side.

"Are we going someplace?" Aleecia asked.

"To the moon," Kyle said.

Aleecia giggled. She had never been kissed before and she wasn't sure where to put her hands. He seemed to engulf her entire soul in his mouth; his lips were so huge and billowy. He was kissing her with such a hunger it took her breath away. He held her face in his hands with such urgent joy, she was sure that no one had ever been kissed better than this. Being kissed like this, it was better than Christmas Day, her birthday, and soloing with the church choir all rolled into one.

///

After he had been kissing her for what seemed like forever, she began to wonder if he was ever going to stop. Aleecia sat up. "This was really nice, but I need to go," she said. "I should find Dawn."

"I can drive you home," Kyle said.

"Oh," Aleecia said. She didn't want her friends to think that she had abandoned them. But she wanted to hold onto this feeling for as long as possible. "Sure," she said at last. "That would be great."

Aleecia's mind raced as Kyle put the car into gear and steered deftly with one hand out of the lot and onto the highway. *Is he my boyfriend?* she wondered. *The captain of the football team!* The thought of it gave her goose bumps. She imagined holding hands in the hallway at school, kissing under the stadium bleachers.

"You're awfully quiet," Kyle said.

Aleecia was paralyzed with shyness. She realized she had no idea what to say. *How did I get here? One minute I was checking him out in Big Lots and the next thing I am kissing him in his car. How does this work? Does he really like me? Or does he just think I'm easy?*

She suddenly regretted wearing the halter dress. She should have worn her cut-offs.

Kyle rested his hand, palm up, in her lap. "Hey," he said. "I really like you."

Aleecia rested her hand lightly in his and they drove the rest of the way in silence.

Four

KYLE

O N SUNDAY MORNING, KYLE SLEPT LATE AND THEN LAY in his bed for a while, scanning his messages on his phone.

Steve texted, What time r u picking us up for the bbq?

Kyle replied, Party starts at 4. You want to get there around 4:30 or 5?

Pick us up at 4:30

Cool

//

"Where are you going?" his mother screamed as the screen door slammed. "I didn't say you could go out. Who is going to watch these babies?"

"Bye, Mama," Kyle yelled over his shoulder.

He jumped into his battered Cavalier and spun out of the gravel driveway.

"Stay home with your babies, bitch," Kyle said, bitterly into the rear view mirror. He cranked up WJFP on the radio and drove fast down Route 1, slowing instinctively for the speed trap across from the FPL substation. As he rolled by in what felt like slow motion, he nodded in the direction of the police cruiser that was idling in the parking lot. A few more miles down the road, he pulled up in front of Steve's house. Steve was the running back on the football team and Kyle's closest friend. Kyle honked the horn and three boys came spilling out of the front door and piled into Kyle's car, dissing each other loudly.

"Pop the trunk!" Steve yelled. He was carrying a cooler.

Kyle got out to open the trunk. "You boys started the party without me?" he asked with a broad smile.

"We raided my mom's liquor cabinet," Steve said. "She won't notice that we watered the vodka down."

"You got anything for me?" Kyle asked.

Steve handed him a flask and Kyle took a deep gulp.

"Bogart!" one of the boys in the back seat yelled.

"Hey!" Kyle yelled back. "You don't need to ride in my car. I can drop you at the gas station on the corner. It's only mile or so to walk to the beach."

//

Kyle pulled into the beach parking lot and walked around to open the trunk.

"I got it," Steve said and lifted the cooler onto his shoulder.

They joined the rest of the football team, who had gathered around a picnic table under an oak tree. The table was laden with buckets of KFC and six-packs of Mountain Dew.

Cars pulled into the lot in a steady stream as the park filled with kids spreading out blankets, coolers, and portable music players. An offshore breeze kicked up and lessened the heat of the day.

Kyle and Steve tossed a football back and forth and a bunch of the other players joined them in a game of two-hand touch.

///

Kyle was just exiting the park restroom when he saw Aleecia jump out of the pickup. The breeze blew her hair in her face and whipped her dress up to show a little bit of panty.

"Damn, I'd tap that." Kyle heard Steve's voice behind him.

"Watch it," Kyle said, "Aleecia is a nice girl."

"You don't even know her," Steve protested.

"We've met," Kyle said. He walked toward her, calling out," Yo."

She looked happy to see him.

"I wasn't sure you were coming," Kyle said. "Want to take a walk on the beach?"

Kyle took her hand and led her down toward the water. The sun was behind them and the air was cool.

Kyle put his arm around Aleecia's shoulder. He could feel the goose bumps on her arm. "Are you cold?"

"I should have brought a sweater," Aleecia said.

"Do you want to go sit in my car?" Kyle said.

"Sure," she said.

Kyle took her hand and led her back to the parking lot. He opened the passenger door for her and then walked around to the driver's side.

"Are we going someplace?" Aleecia asked.

"It's just warmer in here," Kyle said. He pulled her closer to him. "You look really pretty."

"Do you like my dress?" Aleecia asked.

"I do," Kyle said. "Do you want something to drink?" He pulled the flask out from under the seat.

"What is it?" she asked.

"Taste it and see if you like it," Kyle said.

Aleecia took a sip. "It's good," she said.

"I bet it doesn't taste any better than you," Kyle said. "Can I kiss you?"

Aleecia didn't reply so he leaned in and inhaled her. *Her skin is so soft*, he thought. *Her is hair so silky; she smells like a fragrant oasis. I want her to carry me far away—to someplace that doesn't smell like piss and rotten garbage. A place where there are no scared and hungry kids clinging to me like they are drowning and I am their life raft, I am their only hope. I want to go to a place where we can love each other and build a bulwark together; protection from the poverty and violence that wants to tear me down. What is it that she tastes like? She tastes like hope.*

He was just starting to lose himself in the fantasy when she suddenly sat upright.

"This was really nice, but I need to go," she said. "I should find Dawn."

Really? You need to find Dawn? Dawn can take care of herself. Don't leave me. I need you. You are my life raft.

"I can drive you home," Kyle said. He rested his hand, palm up, in her lap. "Hey," he said. "I really like you."

Aleecia rested her hand lightly in his and they drove the rest of the way in silence.

Kyle pulled up in front of Aleecia's house.

"Thank you," Aleecia said. "I had a nice time."

"See you tomorrow?" Kyle asked.

"At school?" Aleecia asked. "Sure."

"Maybe after school?' Kyle said. "I'm done with practice around seven."

"You have football practice in May?" Aleecia asked.

"Spring practice," Kyle said. "Coach asked me to assist. "

"I work on Mondays," Aleecia said.

This is going to be difficult. He was frustrated.

"Okay, you tell me when," Kyle said, and gave her his cell number.

"Would you like to come to church next Sunday?" Aleecia said.

"Church?" Kyle chuckled. *I've never dated anyone who went to church! This is going to be awkward,* he thought.

"I sing in the choir, I mean," Aleecia said.

"I'd like that," Kyle said, relieved. "To hear you sing."

Five

ALEECIA

"**M**OM, I'M HOME," ALEECIA CALLED OUT. HER SKIN tingled with the lingering memory of sand and salt spray from the ocean. She longed for the embrace of Kyle's arms, his musky smell. *This has been the best day of my life*, she thought. *I never want this feeling to end!*

Her mom came into the living room, a bottle of beer in her hand, still wearing her home aid uniform.

"You won't believe my day," her mother said. "Mrs. Flanagan called the cops on me again today. She claimed that I was stealing from her. I had to explain to the officer that I was her home aid. My supervisor had to come down on her day off to intervene. What a shit show."

She took a sip from her bottle and looked hard at Aleecia.

"Where have you been? What is that you are wearing?" her mother asked.

"This is Gina's dress. I went to a party on the beach. There were a bunch of kids from school."

"You went to the beach in that?"

"Gina said I looked beautiful," Aleecia said.

"You look cheap," her mother said. "That dress is too tight—you look like a stuffed sausage."

"Stuffed sausage? Mom!" Aleecia cried. She looked at her reflection in the hall mirror and her face fell. The wind had blown her hair into knots; her mascara had formed raccoon rings under her eyes, and her dress was bunched up around her too-thick waist. *What does Kyle see in me?*

"Was there a boy involved?" her mother asked.

"Kyle is the captain of the football team," Aleecia said. "He invited me."

"This boy, Kyle?" she said. "He didn't touch you."

"Touch me?" Aleecia said.

"Aleecia, baby," her mother said. "You're fifteen. You're too young to start running around with boys. I'm going to have a word with Gina. Dressing you up like a slut and sending you out to the beach. How old is this boy?"

"Kyle is a senior," Aleecia said.

"He's too old for you," her mother said.

"I don't understand," Aleecia said.

"Exactly," her mother said. "You don't understand. You're too young for this. You need to stay in school. You're going to college. I don't want you ending up like me—single mom, working for an hourly wage, scraping by. I want a better life for you. Go wash that makeup off of your face. Did you do your homework?"

"Yes, Mama," Aleecia said.

Aleecia changed into a T-shirt and pajama bottoms, tied back her hair, and scrubbed her face. She gazed at her reflection in the mirror and thought about how it felt when Kyle kissed her. *That was the happiest I've ever been*, she said to herself in the mirror.

Aleecia climbed into bed and pulled out her diary.

Dear Diary,

Today was the best day ever. Kyle saw me the minute I got to the beach and never left my side. Everyone was watching us. Me! With the captain of the football team! Please, God, let this be real. Let him be my boyfriend. My first boyfriend. That feeling when he held me in his arms and swallowed me in his kiss—such a feeling of love and passion and anticipation— now I know. This is the point of everything.

Kyle

After Kyle dropped Aleecia at home, he drove back to the park to find Steve and the others. They had built a roaring bonfire on the beach that he could see from a mile away. The park was mostly deserted and trash was strewn everywhere. Taking sips from the flask, he made his way over to the fire pit. He recognized Steve and the rest of the posse along with Jordan and Janelle and a few of the other cheerleaders.

"Hey, Romeo!" Steve called out. "Where's Cinderella?"

"Who's Cinderella?" Janelle asked.

"Some freshman he was hitting on," Jordan said. "I guess she had to be home before dark." The girls giggled.

Janelle shot Kyle a jealous look. "Seriously, Kyle. You're dating a child?" she taunted.

Ignoring them, Kyle plopped down on the cold sand next to Steve and just as he did, his phone vibrated in his pocket. He pulled it out, hoping to see Aleecia's number. But the caller ID read "Lucifer," his pet name for his mother. He sighed deeply as he answered, "What is it?"

"Where are you?" his mother sounded drunk. "I've been calling you for hours."

"No, Ma," Kyle said. "There are no calls from you. You must have been calling somebody else."

"I need you to come home," she said. "Dwayne is hungry."

"So feed him." Kyle could hear Crystal crying in the background. "What's wrong with the baby?"

"I don't have any food in the house," she said. "Pick up some KFC for the kids. When are you coming home?"

"I'll be there," Kyle said and hung up.

"Gotta go," Kyle said to Steve. "Anybody need a ride?"

"No, thanks man," Steve said.

Kyle knew Aleecia wouldn't be working, so he swung by the Big Lots to pick up formula, hot dogs, cereal, milk and some frozen mac and cheese, putting them all on the SNAP card.

When he got home, the house was dark. He could make out his mother's silhouette on the couch.

"FPL cut us off again?" Kyle asked.

"What did you bring me, baby?" his mom asked.

"Just some food for the kids," he said. In the kitchen, he found a candle and held it to the gas burner on the stove to light it. He boiled some water and went outside to retrieve the spent cooler from his trunk. There was still some ice left so he plunged the milk carton in and closed the lid tight.

Kyle woke up Crystal to change her and give her a bottle. He put a plate of mac and cheese and hot dogs drenched in ketchup on a tray and carried it into Dwayne.

"Hey, buddy," Kyle said. "Are you hungry?"

Dwayne sat up on his bed, rubbing his eyes. "KFC?"

"Even better," Kyle said and set the tray down on the floor.

Kyle sat on the floor and scooped Dwayne into his lap. He felt guilty for running off that morning, escaping to the beach to hang with his friends and hook up with Aleecia. Dwayne scarfed down the food as Kyle cuddled him, wishing it were Aleecia in his arms.

Six

ALEECIA

ALEECIA WOKE UP EARLY ON MONDAY MORNING; SHE was eager to get to school. She washed and styled her hair, in an attempt to look like Rihanna.

"What are you doing in there so long?" her mother tapped on the bathroom door. "I need to leave for work."

Aleecia opened the door. "Mama, can you help me with my hair?"

"What's wrong with your hair?" her mother asked.

"I want to look pretty," Aleecia said.

"You always look pretty, baby," her mother said

with a chuckle as she took the hairbrush from Aleecia. "Hand me the hairspray."

Aleecia looked at her mother's reflection in the mirror and smiled. "Remember when I was little and you would fix up my hair so fancy for church?"

Her mother looked up and their eyes met in the mirror. "I wish I could do this every day, baby," her mother said, tearing up. "If I didn't have to work such long hours. Pretty soon, you'll be all grown up and gone." She leaned down and kissed the top of Aleecia's head. "Let me pee. I'm going to be late."

///

Aleecia dawdled at her locker, hoping to see Kyle before the eight-twenty bell rang. She was about to give up when she heard his voice down the hall. A posse of football players surrounded him. She suddenly felt shy and walked quickly in the opposite direction. She made it to class on time but had difficulty concentrating; she thought about him all day and wondered if he was thinking about her.

At lunch she met up with Dawn and Joyce, and they found an empty picnic table in the courtyard.

"Spill it," Joyce said. "What happened with Kyle? What's he like?"

Aleecia's face grew hot as she thought about how it felt to be so close to him, how he smelled. "He's nice."

"Nice?" Joyce said. "C'mon, he's the captain of the football team. He's probably going to Tallahassee and then on to play for the Dolphins. Am I right?"

"I guess," Aleecia said.

"You need to be careful, girl," Dawn said. "How do you know he isn't using you?"

The bell rang and they collected their trash, grabbed their backpacks, and headed inside. Aleecia saw Kyle standing by the door. The back of her neck tingled with excitement. *Was he waiting there for me?* she wondered.

"Aleecia," Kyle said.

Dawn and Joyce pushed past Aleecia, jostling her deliberately. Aleecia giggled.

"Can I give you a ride home after work?" Kyle said.

"Sure," Aleecia said. "I mean, I'm not sure if I'll be off at eight or nine."

"Text me when you know for sure," he said.

//

After her shift had ended, Aleecia walked her bike to the front parking lot. She saw Kyle parked in the far corner and felt his eyes on her as she wheeled her bike over.

"This is really nice of you," she said to him as he loaded her bike into the trunk.

"It's not safe for you to ride home in the dark," he said. "I worry about you."

He's worrying about me? she thought. Aleecia didn't know what to say.

They drove with the windows down, enjoying the salty breeze. Kyle reached out for her hand and held it gently, resting it on his thigh. *This feels so intimate!*

"How was practice?" Aleecia asked.

Kyle responded with a long-winded litany of details about players and plays, none of which she understood.

I love the sound of his voice, she thought. Aleecia leaned back in the passenger seat and smiled contentedly through the open window at the reflection of the moon on the restless waves cresting in the distance.

Kyle pulled up in front of her house and parked.

"Are you still coming to church on Sunday?" Aleecia said. *Church is the most important thing in my life and I want it to be important to him, too*, she thought.

"Church? Oh, right. Yes," he said. "I'll come." He was still holding her hand. "Can I have a kiss?"

Aleecia leaned in and inhaled. He smelled earthy and spicy. His lips formed pillows for hers.

Kyle

On Monday, Kyle kept hoping to run into Aleecia at school. He passed by her locker several times. Finally he spotted her, but Steve and the guys were there, acting like asses. He watched as she closed her locker and walked away. He was overcome with a desire to talk to her, to make sure she was really there, that she was into him, that maybe she could save him.

He mentally mapped her movements all day and finally saw an opening at lunch. She usually sat outside with her friends. He positioned himself by the door to the hallway where she had her fifth-period class and waited.

"Aleecia," Kyle said. "Can I give you a ride home after work?" *Do I sound desperate?* he wondered. She seemed happy to see him. "Text me when you know what time you are getting off."

That evening, Kyle sat in the parking lot of Big Lots until all the customers had left and the streetlights had come on. *Is she still coming?* he wondered. Then he saw a dark figure wheeling a bike toward him. He jumped out to pop the trunk and load up her bike.

"This is really nice of you," she said.

"I wanted you to be safe," he said.

As he drove down the highway, he reached out for her hand and held it gently, resting it on his thigh.

"How was work?" Kyle asked.

Aleecia responded with a long-winded story about her coworkers and some nonsense about annoying customers, none of whom he knew.

Kyle relaxed and smiled contentedly as she prattled on, cherishing the warmth of her hand in his.

Kyle pulled up in front of her house and parked.

"Don't forget about church on Sunday," Aleecia said.

"I won't," he said. He pulled her toward him and kissed her. He wanted the kiss to last forever, an endless feast for his hungry soul, a banquet that he had finally been invited to.

Every day that week, Kyle looked for Aleecia, lurking around her locker, hoping to catch her coming and going. Each time he did, she reminded him: "See you at church on Sunday." *Oh, my God*, he thought, *what is it with her and church?*

Seven

ALEECIA

WHEN SHE WOKE UP THE FOLLOWING SUNDAY, ALEECIA was a wreck. Her throat was sore; her hair wouldn't behave. She wanted everything to be perfect. She left early so she could ride her bike slowly. She didn't want to show up all sweaty and disheveled. She joined the other choir members in the rehearsal room where they warmed up and went over the order of service.

"Aleecia, can you sing the first verse as a solo?" Mr. Buckles said, "And then the chorus will join in."

She had been asked to sing solo many times, but this

time was different. Kyle would be there to hear her. Half of her was thrilled, the other half was terrified.

As the choir filed into the church and took their places in front of the altar, Aleecia looked out into the sea of faces, hoping to see Kyle. *He's not here! He didn't come!* she lamented.

The organ struck a chord. Nerves assuaged, her muscle memory took over and Aleecia sang "Ubi Caritas et Amor" in a deep alto voice. She felt the notes resonating in her gut and lifted her head to project the sound to the rafters. When the hymn was over, the congregation erupted in applause.

//

Kyle was waiting for Aleecia outside the church after the service.

"You came!" Aleecia croaked. Her voice was hoarse from singing. She stood on her toes and reached up to kiss him.

"Of course I came," he said. "You sang like an

angel," Kyle said, squeezing her hand in his fist. "That was amazing! The lady sitting next to me told me that you were the best singer in the choir. Do you have time to go for a walk on the beach?" he asked.

Kyle loaded Aleecia's bike into his trunk and drove to the beach parking lot. He parked and walked around to open the passenger door. Aleecia took his hand.

"My lady," Kyle said.

He led her down to the sand where she stopped to remove her sandals.

They walked hand-in-hand southward along the beach, the sun baking them in its warmth.

"I have this crazy dream," she said. "I want to be a famous gospel singer. I want to move to Nashville and get rich and famous."

"That's a great dream," he said. "There is so much I want to accomplish, too."

"You mean football, right?" she asked. "Is that going to be your career?"

"That's right. NFL, baby. Money fixes everything, right?" he asked. "Get ourselves out of this hellhole."

"Nashville has a football team, doesn't it?" she asked.

He laughed. "The Titans. You become a famous gospel singer, and I'll play for the Titans."

"I'm serious," she said.

"I know you're serious," he said. "That was serious shit today, in church."

"We can do this, right?"

"Well," Kyle hesitated. "I need to take care of my little brother and sister. Do you have sisters and brothers?"

"No, it's just me and my mom," Aleecia said. "I never knew my daddy. She never talks about him."

"You're lucky," Kyle said. "If it weren't for them, I'd be able to leave. Dwayne is eight and baby Crystal is two."

"Where would you go?" Aleecia asked.

"I've never talked to anybody about this before," Kyle said. "I'd go far away, maybe Atlanta."

Aleecia squeezed Kyle's hand and he stopped and turned to face her.

"Would you like to go to the prom with me?"

Aleecia gasped. "Senior prom?" *This is the best day ever,* she thought. *He came to my church and he asked me to his prom!* "Yes, yes, yes!"

"Give me a kiss," he said.

Aleecia stood on tiptoe to reach his lips.

They walked along the beach, the sand swallowing her feet and grinding in between her toes. She imagined tracing their names into the sand, *Aleecia & Kyle 4Ever. We'll move to Tennessee and he'll play for the Titans. I'll rocket up the charts with a cameo on* Nashville. *We'll have a big house, just like on the TV show, and my mama and his family would live with us.* She squeezed his hand at the thought.

Kyle

That morning, Kyle had gotten up early to run a load of laundry. Dwayne poked his head in from the kitchen.

"Where are you going?" Dwayne asked.

"How do you know I'm going somewhere?" Kyle said.

"Why are you up doing laundry, then?" Dwayne asked.

"I'm going to church," Kyle said and laughed.

"Is there food at church?" Dwayne asked. "Can I go?"

Kyle looked into Dwayne's eyes, which were massive. They took up half of the room. *Will there ever be enough food in the world for Dwayne?* he wondered.

"A girl from school asked me to come see her sing," Kyle said. "I don't think they have food, just music and long, boring speeches. You wouldn't like it."

//

Kyle had never been in a church before. He stood on the sidewalk and watched the people as they gathered and greeted each other. Then, just before eleven o'clock, everyone started to file inside. He joined the line and followed the crowd inside. He found a seat near the back and glanced around him to figure out what he was supposed to do. The woman next to him was leafing through a prayer book. He folded his hands and stared straight ahead. Then he saw Aleecia walk through a door to the right of the altar, followed by the rest of the choir. The music started and a lone voice rang out. He craned his neck to see who was singing—*it's Aleecia!* His jaw dropped, and he must have made a sound because the woman next to him was looking at him.

"Sorry," he whispered. "That's my . . . friend."

"Our Aleecia?" she whispered back. "She's quite a talent!"

//

After the service, Kyle waited outside on the sidewalk. When he saw Aleecia, he waved.

"You sang like an angel," he said, embracing her. "What are you doing now? Do you have time for a walk on the beach?"

//

They picked their way carefully along the water line,
avoiding trash, broken glass, discarded syringes and
condoms.

"Happy?" she asked.

Kyle burned with shame. *What can I tell her about
my life?* he thought. *That the kids are always hungry, or
about FPL shutting off the power again last night? She
only knows me as the football team captain. Nobody knows
about the other stuff. Or I least I hope that no one knows.*

"What about you?" Kyle said, changing the subject.
"What do you want to do when you grow up?"

"Nashville," she said.

"The TV show?" he asked.

"Both," she said. "The city and the show. I want
to be famous."

"I'm sure you will be," he said. "The NFL is my
ticket out of here."

"Where would you go?" Aleecia asked.

Kyle had never told anyone his dreams before. The

local college scouts, Florida State and University of Florida, came to his games, but he wanted to get as far away as possible. "Maybe Atlanta," he said. *But what about Dwayne and baby Crystal?* he thought. *I can't abandon them.* He imagined moving to Atlanta with Aleecia—they'd find a two-bedroom apartment with room for Dwayne and Crystal.

He stopped and faced her. "You wouldn't want to go to prom, would you? I wasn't planning on going but it's my last year here and maybe you'd want to go with me?"

Aleecia gasped and jumped up and down in front of him. "Yes, yes, yes!"

Eight

ALEECIA

ALEECIA SAT ON THE PORCH, WAITING FOR HER MOTHER to get home from work. When the battered Ford pulled into the driveway, she jumped up and ran.

"Mama, I'm going to the prom!" Aleecia danced and spun around in the driveway.

"Prom?" her mother asked. "You're a freshman."

"Kyle asked me to senior prom," Aleecia said.

"That boy?" her mother said. "You're still seeing him?"

"Mama, it's not what you think," Aleecia

protested. "He's been coming to church. And we go for walks on the beach. He's a nice boy. You would like him."

"He goes to our church?" her mother said. "Do I know his family?"

"You work on Sundays," Aleecia said. "When was the last time you were at church?"

"True," her mother said. "Well, if they go to our church, I guess it's okay."

Aleecia felt bad about lying to her mother and hoped she wouldn't go to hell for it. But she was in love with Kyle, and he'd asked her to prom! Then she started to panic. *The prom is on Friday! Am I supposed to work that day?* she wondered. *Did I remember to tell Mr. Martin about the prom?*

That evening as she clocked in, Aleecia scanned the schedule. She was relieved to see that she was not scheduled for Friday. But just to be safe, she took out a pen and drew a big X in the schedule by her name to indicate to Mr. Martin that she wasn't available as a backup.

///

The next morning, Aleecia asked her mother, "What
will I wear to the prom?"

Her mother rested her hip against the kitchen
counter and cradled her coffee mug.

"Sweetie, you know I would love to sew you something pretty, but I gotta work all week," her mother
said. "I'll ask my sister, Rosa, to make you a dress.
What color are you thinking? Pink?"

"Maybe yellow?"

"Satin?" her mother said.

"Yes!" Aleecia said.

///

The next day, Rosa took Aleecia to Jo-Ann's Fabrics
pick out a pattern.

"What are we thinking, strapless?" Aunt Rosa
asked as she thumbed through the dress patterns.

"No, I'd be worrying all night about my dress slipping," Aleecia said. "How about spaghetti straps?"

Rosa flipped through a few more boxes. "I found a couple of nice dresses. Take a look," she said.

Aleecia held up the dress patterns. "I'll look like a princess!" she said.

Rosa took the patterns back and read the backs. "Let's see which one requires less fabric. Go pick out some fabric. Your mother said something about pink."

Aleecia wandered the aisles of fabrics and found the Silks & Satins section. She picked out a bolt of canary-yellow satin and carried it back to where Rosa was looking at zippers and thread.

"I thought we agreed on pink?" Rosa asked.

"I want yellow," Aleecia said. "It sparkles like gold."

///

The next three days were a blur of sewing and fitting sessions as the dress took shape.

"What about your hair, nails and makeup?" Rosa asked.

"I don't know," Aleecia said. "I guess my mom will help me?"

"Oh, no, no, no," Rosa said. "Your cousin Rita works in a salon. She can do it." Rosa picked up her cell phone and started to dial. "You will look fabulous."

"Rita!" Rosa shouted into the phone. "It's your mother! Aleecia is going to the prom and I need you to doll her up—hair, nails, makeup—the whole works."

Aleecia looked down at her nails, which were chipped and cracked, and smiled to herself. She so desperately wanted to look beautiful for the prom, for Kyle.

"Okay, then," Rosa said. "The prom is Friday, we'll bring her after school. Thank you, sweetie. Bye-bye." Rosa hung up the phone.

"That's settled then," Rosa said. "Friday after school, go over to Rita's shop."

The week seemed to drag on forever. Aleecia could not pay attention in class. Finally, it was Friday and when the final bell rang, she hopped on her bike and pedaled to her cousin Rita's beauty shop on Second Street.

Inside, Aleecia faced a cacophony of hairdryers and women shouting over them.

"Hey, little sister," Rita said. "Look at you—you're all grown up."

Rita led Aleecia to a nail stand. "Nails first, then hair, then makeup—okay?"

Aleecia settled in the chair and presented her hands for inspection.

"Did you pick a color?" Rita said.

"My dress is yellow—lemon yellow," Aleecia said.

"Okay, OPI's *Need Sunglasses*, here we go," Rita said.

//

Aleecia was admiring her nails as Rita led her to the hairdresser station.

"What are we thinking, do you want your hair up or down?" Rita asked.

"I like my hair down," Aleecia said.

"Blow-out and curling iron, yes?" Rita asked.

It was already five o'clock and Aleecia was getting antsy. She could no longer sit still as Rita meticulously fluffed and smoothed her hair this way and that.

"My ass is killing me," Aleecia said. "Are we done?" She immediately felt bad about sounding rude.

"Look in the mirror, baby," Rita said. "Tell me what you think."

Aleecia opened her eyes and was overcome. "I look so beautiful! Thank you!" She started to cry.

"No, no, no," Rita said. "You'll ruin it. No crying!"

///

Aleecia sat on the couch flipping through channels and eyeing the clock. *Where is he?* she wondered.

Then she heard his car.

"Mommy!" Aleecia cried. "He's here."

Kyle came to the door in a dark suit.

The photos that Aleecia's mother took would later show Kyle anxiously clutching a corsage that he would fumble with as he fastened it to Aleecia's dress. And Aleecia's knuckles were white as she gripped Kyle's hand hard.

In the car, Kyle said, "You look nice. Do you want some?" He brandished a flask.

"What is it?" Aleecia asked.

"Jack Daniels," Kyle said. "Try it."

Aleecia took the flask and raised it to her lips. It burned. And then the warmth spread through her neck and shoulders, relaxing her. She took another sip and then another.

The rest of the evening was a blur. She remembered dancing and Kyle holding her tight. She remembered kissing him and getting sick in the bathroom. And then the gym lights came on.

"Is it over?" Aleecia asked.

"Let's go to the after-party," Kyle said. "At the Days Inn. I got us a room."

Aleecia was too woozy to argue. She needed to lie down.

///

Aleecia sat in the car while Kyle checked them in. It took so long that she had started to fall asleep and was startled when he opened her door.

"Let's go," he said.

He took Aleecia's hand and led her to room 108. Aleecia knew she would be in trouble with her mother but she was too tired to care. She let Kyle undress her and lay her down on the bed. What came next shocked and surprised her. She was no longer a princess being cherished. He pressed himself into her. It hurt. She didn't expect this. In a few minutes it was over and he collapsed next to her, snoring, cradling her breast in his hand.

Suddenly she was wide-awake and couldn't sleep. *What was I expecting? I drank too much at the prom. He booked a motel room—of course he had it all planned out. But I didn't feel like I could say no. It was prom night. Everyone was doing it, right?*

In the morning, Aleecia kissed Kyle awake. "My mom sleeps late on Saturday. We need to get there before she wakes up."

"I'm sorry about last night," he said. "I want this to be good for you."

Kyle was hard again and thrust himself into her. *This is sex?* Aleecia thought. *Seriously? This is what the big deal is all about? I don't think I like this.*

//

They dressed in silence. Aleecia was suddenly aware of how it would look, her in her prom gown, walking down the sidewalk of the motel. "The walk of shame," she said. She let out a little laugh.

"Everything okay?" Kyle asked.

"Um," Aleecia said. "I was a virgin, you know?"

"You wanted to do it, right?" Kyle said. "I wouldn't have done anything unless you wanted to."

"No, of course," Aleecia said. "I just wish I had brought a change of clothes."

"I thought I told you about the motel?" Kyle asked.

"I guess?" Aleecia said. "I don't remember."

Kyle pulled Aleecia to him. "I love you, baby," he said.

"Me too," she said.

///

Kyle pulled his car into Aleecia's driveway and stopped short. Her mother stood on the front porch, arms folded.

"Where have you been?" her mother demanded. "I called you."

"You called me?" Aleecia said. "I was out with Joyce all night."

"I called Joyce's mother," her mother said. "She was home by one."

"Shit," Kyle said.

"That's it, you're grounded," her mother said.

Aleecia turned to Kyle. "I'm sorry about this," she said. "My mother . . . "

"I know," Kyle said. "You don't have to say anything. I'll see you tomorrow? At church?"

Nine

KYLE

EVER SINCE HE HAD AGREED TO TAKE ALEECIA TO THE prom, Kyle had been worried about what he would wear. He didn't want his mother to know that he was going—she would just ridicule him and call Aleecia nasty names. A whistle blew indicating that practice was over, and Steve approached him.

"Hey, does your brother, Woody, still work at that fancy hotel in Vero Beach?" Kyle asked.

"Yeah, why?" Steve said.

"I need something to wear to prom," Kyle said. "Do you think I could borrow a suit from him?"

"Prom? Seriously?" Steve punched Kyle. "Why the hell would you want to go to prom?"

"Aleecia wants to go," Kyle said. "It's my last year—her last chance, is the way she put it. So would Woody lend me a suit?"

"I guess so," Steve said. "I can ask him."

When word spread through the team that Kyle was taking Aleecia to prom, some of the other players decided to go too and they booked rooms at the Days Inn for an after-party.

The party started at sundown on the beach and the boys were drinking beers and passing around a flask of whiskey.

Kyle was pretty buzzed when he arrived at Aleecia's house. He took a swig of mouthwash and spat it out onto the driveway before popping a couple of Altoids.

Nervously, he reached for the doorbell as the door swung open. Aleecia stood in the doorway; the light from the hallway formed a halo around her and illuminated her in a golden gown.

"Wow," Kyle said. "You look like angel."

"Come in." Aleecia tugged at his hand. "My mom wants to take a picture."

Kyle followed her inside. The living room was tidy and all the colors were coordinated, unlike the mismatched thrift-store look of his house.

"Mom, this is Kyle," Aleecia said.

Kyle extended his hand in greeting.

"Nice to meet you, Kyle," her mother said. "Don't you look handsome? Oh, and you brought a corsage!"

While her mom snapped photos, Kyle fumbled with the corsage and pinned it to Aleecia's dress. Then they posed side by side for more photos until Aleecia became impatient.

"C'mon," she said. "We're going to be late. Don't wait up, Mom."

They walked out holding hands, her dress rustling as she walked.

"Isn't this exciting?" she said.

Kyle scooped up the flask from the passenger seat so Aleecia could sit.

"Have you been drinking?" Aleecia asked.

"The guys were hanging out on the beach," he said.

"Can I have a sip?" she asked.

///

Aleecia was pretty wasted by the time they got to the dance. Kyle doubted she'd remember much about the evening. It seemed to him like she spent most of the dance in the bathroom. Then the gym lights came on and they could finally get out of there.

"Did you have fun?" Kyle said as he steadied her on the way to the car.

She mumbled something.

Kyle poured her into the passenger seat and steered toward the beach.

"Where are we going now?" Aleecia said. "This isn't the way home."

"After-party," he said. "Remember?"

//

Aleecia was passed out in the front seat of the car when Kyle returned with the hotel key. *I guess we're skipping the party*, he thought.

He took her hand and helped her into the room, locking the door behind him.

She flopped down on to the bed.

"Aleecia, honey," he said. "Do you want to get undressed?"

She mumbled something. He gently rolled her over on her side, unzipped her dress and slid it over her shoulders and around her hips. He pulled down her panties and gazed at her. *Oh, man, she is hot!* he thought. *I wish she would wake up so we could do it.*

"Aleecia, are you awake?" he asked. He hurriedly stripped down. He switched off the lamp but left the bathroom light on with the door cracked open.

"What?" she asked. She opened her eyes a crack

and seemed to be watching him as he fumbled with a condom.

"Are you ready?" Kyle asked. "I don't want to hurt you."

Aleecia didn't say anything.

Kyle spread her legs, entered her and came almost immediately.

"Shit," he said, rolling over to her side. "I'm sorry, baby." But she was already out cold again. He pulled her close to him and cradled her in his arms all night.

///

In the morning, Kyle awoke to Aleecia kissing him.

"Hey, wake up, baby," Aleecia said. "I need to get home before my mom wakes up," Aleecia said.

"I'm sorry about last night," he said. "I wanted our first time to be good for you. We have time, right?" He pulled out a condom and started to unwrap it.

"What are you doing?" she said.

"Get on top," he said.

"No," she protested. But she was giggling so he slipped on the condom and pulled her onto him. He studied her face but he couldn't tell if she was enjoying it.

When he finished she tried to pull away and he held her tightly in his arms.

"No, really, we gotta go," Aleecia said. "My mom sleeps late on Saturday. We need to get there before she wakes up or there will be hell to pay."

They dressed hastily and Aleecia waited in the car while Kyle checked out.

//

As Kyle turned the corner onto Aleecia's street he saw her mother standing in the driveway and his heart jumped into his throat. This would not end well.

Kyle sat in the car and watched Aleecia follow her mother into the house. He could see them through the front window, her mother gesturing wildly and Aleecia covering her face with her hands. He expected her mom to haul back and slap Aleecia, and he was surprised to see Aleecia fall into her mom's arms. He felt bad for Aleecia, but mostly he felt jealous. *Aleecia and her mom are so close,* he thought. He had never known that kind of feeling. He had never had someone get angry because they wanted to protect him.

They moved out of view and he drove slowly home, thinking about the night before. He'd planned it as a romantic evening; it was anything but that. He realized he probably should have taken her straight home from the dance. *This wasn't how I wanted our first time to be. I wonder if I'll get a chance to make it right.*

Ten

KYLE

WHEN HE GOT HOME FROM DROPPING ALEECIA OFF, Kyle was relieved to find the house empty. He took a quick shower and changed into gym shorts. He poured a bowl of Honey-Nut Cheerios and sniffed the carton of milk before deciding that it was okay. He plopped onto the couch and, holding the bowl in his left hand, surfed the TV with his right and landed on Cartoon Network: The Scooby-Doo movie. *Perfect!*

He fell asleep on the couch and was jolted awake by Dwayne climbing onto him.

"Wake up!" Dwayne said.

Kyle rubbed his eyes. "What time is it? Where have you been?"

"Aunt Georgia's house," Dwayne said.

"Where's your mama?" Kyle asked.

"Jared came and picked her and Crystal up," Dwayne said.

"Jared?" Kyle was wide-awake now. "That asshole is back in the picture?" Sure, Jared was Crystal's daddy, but he was an addict, and all the trouble with Mom started when she met him.

"I guess," Dwayne said.

"Are you hungry?" Kyle asked. "What am I saying— you're always hungry, right, little dude?"

As he fixed a bowl of cereal for Dwayne, he thought about Aleecia and wondered what she was doing.

He texted her. Everything OK?

Aleecia replied, I'm grounded for a month. I'm not supposed to be texting with you. Gotta go.

Shit, that's not right, Kyle thought. *We love each other—her mom can't keep us from seeing each other. I need to see her. School's almost over and then what? I can still see her at Big Lots—unless me hanging around gets her in trouble with her boss. Better yet, I can drive her home. That's it; I'll offer to drive her home every night. Her mom doesn't need to know.*

//

Kyle stayed up late, watching TV, and overslept on Sunday morning.

"Shit, shit, shit," he said as he scrambled to find clothes that didn't stink.

Dwayne walked in from the kitchen. He had a milk mustache and food stains on his pajama top.

"Where are you going?" Dwayne asked. "Can I come?"

"I gotta get to church," Kyle said. "I'm late. And, no, you can't come. Maybe someday."

The doors were closed when Kyle arrived at the church. He didn't know what to do, so he sat in his car and waited for the service to end. He nodded off and only awoke when he heard loud voices. The street was full of people, some of them were resting against his car.

"'Scuse, me," Kyle said as he forced his door open.

He was scared that he had missed her. Then he saw Aleecia coming down the front steps. She scanned the crowd. She's looking for me, he thought. He waved. She stood still, staring at him from a distance. *What's going on?* he wondered.

"Aleecia!" he yelled again.

She walked slowly across the street toward him.

"How are you, baby?" Kyle said.

"Look, you can't be here. I'm not supposed to see you for a month."

"Your mom's not around," Kyle said. "She works on Sunday, right? And besides, who is going to tell her?" He reached for her hand but she took a step back.

"No, but I need her to trust me again," Aleecia said. "As if that were possible."

"Are you mad at me?" he asked.

"Yes . . . no . . . maybe?" she said. "I don't know; I

just feel so guilty. I've never lied to my mother before. And I know she knows I lied and I'm afraid she'll never trust me again."

"I need to see you," he said. "Aleecia, I love you, you know that, right? What happened on Friday—I never meant to hurt you. I thought you wanted it too."

"How can you say that?" Aleecia asked. "I had too much to drink; I needed to lie down. I remember that part. The rest of it—I don't feel good about it. You're going to think this sounds stupid, but I don't feel right in the eyes of the Lord."

In the eyes of the Lord? Kyle thought. *I didn't know that she took all this church shit so seriously. But that's what I love about her—her purity, her earnestness. She is all heart and that's just the kind of girl I want to marry.*

"It's not stupid," he said. "That's a big part of what I love about you. I need your mom to know that."

"You love me?" Aleecia asked. "You really love me?"

"Yes, baby," *And I do. I've never felt this way about anyone before. You make me feel like everything will be all right.*

"I love you, too!" Aleecia exclaimed.

"Kiss me?" Kyle asked.

"We can't let anyone see us together," Aleecia said. She squeezed his hand and turned to walk toward the bike stand.

"Wait! Can I at least give you a ride home after work?" Kyle asked. "Tomorrow night?"

Aleecia stopped and thought about that for a long time. "Um, I guess that would be okay." Aleecia said, eventually. "As long as you drop me a block away from my house and she doesn't see you."

Her expression seemed troubled.

"Hey, your singing was beautiful," he lied.

Aleecia seemed distracted, distant. "Thanks," she said.

He watched her fiddle with her lock on the bike rack. *Damn, her ass is cute!* he thought.

///

Every night that Aleecia was working, Kyle arrived at Big Lots at eight o'clock on the dot. He knew he'd have a wait, so he passed the time playing with his phone, swiping through images on Instagram. There were naked photos of some of the senior girls—selfies they had sent to guys on the football team, who then shared them indiscriminately. There was this one from Karen, the girl in his Sociology class, the one whose freckles on her face and neck ran all the way down to her nipples—he couldn't get that image out of his head. Kyle was fully aroused by the time he saw Aleecia wheeling her bike toward his car.

He made small talk, asking about her day. Doing his best to make her laugh, all the time he was aching, aching for her to touch him. As he approached the usual drop-off spot, two blocks from her house, this time, he didn't want to say goodbye.

"Baby, please," he said. Kyle figured Aleecia had given head before. Girls started doing that in fifth grade.

He kissed her tenderly and then he whispered. "Will you?"

"Will I what?" Aleecia asked.

"Go down on me," Kyle said.

"I don't know how to do that," Aleecia said.

"It's easy," Kyle said, unzipping his pants. "Just like a popsicle."

"I don't know," Aleecia said.

"C'mon, baby," Kyle said. "If you love me."

She didn't seem to know her way around so he helped her a little, guiding her head toward the sweet spot. *Oh that's it, baby! Oh yeah!*

I love you, he thought. Maybe he had said it out loud.

"That was great!" Kyle said.

"Yeah," Aleecia said, wiping her mouth.

He helped her with her bike and then watched her peddle down the dark street toward her house. Mentally, he ticked off the days until she was no longer grounded. He waited until he could no longer see her and then he drove home.

Eleven

ALEECIA

"**W**HERE WERE YOU LAST NIGHT?" ALEECIA'S MOTHER asked. She was standing in the kitchen with her arms folded.

"There was an after-party, Mama," Aleecia said. "I fell asleep. Dawn was there."

"I called Dawn's mother," her mother said. "Dawn was home in bed by midnight. Why are you lying to me?"

"I guess Dawn went home after I fell asleep—but she *was* there, I swear!" Aleecia said.

"You know what happens to girls who fall asleep

at parties?" her mother asked. "They get date-raped. Where was Kyle?"

"Kyle was there," Aleecia said. "He drove me home, remember? If I had planned to stay out all night, don't you think I would have taken a change of clothes? Please, Mama, can I go take a shower and go back to bed? I shouldn't have stayed out. I should have called you. I'm sorry, Mama, I truly am. Can I please not be grounded?"

"No, you're definitely grounded for one month," her mother said. "How do we know that Kyle didn't take advantage of you? What were you wearing when you woke up?"

Aleecia hesitated.

"Oh my God in heaven!" her mother exclaimed. "If he touched you, that's statutory rape. You're under the age of consent. I'm calling the police."

"Don't call the police, Mama," Aleecia pleaded. "Kyle didn't do anything. He calls me his angel. We're planning to get married and move to Nashville."

Her mother's face registered shock.

"Not now, Mama!" Aleecia said. "After I graduate. Of course."

"Well this angel is grounded," her mother said. "Case closed."

"Can I go to church?" Aleecia asked.

"Church, school and work," her mother said. "No boys, no beaches, no parties for one month. And no texting with that boy!"

Aleecia went into the bathroom and turned on the shower. She peeled off her dress and dropped it onto the floor. When she took off her panties, she noticed a little blood stain.

"Oh, shit!" Aleecia said. Frantic, she scrubbed the panties with soap in the sink. If her mother found them she would know that she had lied.

In the shower, she stood under the hot water for a long time, washing off his smell and her memories. Her vagina was sore and she was scared that Kyle had injured her. She had so looked forward to the prom and now she could barely remember dancing with him. She regretted the whole night. It wasn't anything like she had expected. And now she had lost her mother's trust. It would never be the same.

//

At church on Sunday, Aleecia felt different. The music didn't take her soul to a new place; it made her feel unworthy. She felt like she had let Jesus down. She felt like an imposter—a fallen woman. She was shattered. And furious with Kyle. But most of all furious with herself. *I trusted him!* she thought. *I had no idea there actually is a point of no return.*

After the service, she saw Kyle standing on the sidewalk across the street. Her heart leapt into her throat. She wanted to run to him but she had promised her mom. She hoped he hadn't seen her. She wished she could just ride her Rally home alone and somehow turn back the clock, back to before Friday.

"Aleecia!" Kyle yelled and waved.

Aleecia stood there, weighing the risk. She knew she

couldn't be seen with him or her mother would ground her permanently. She walked slowly across the street.

"That was beautiful," Kyle said.

"What was?" Aleecia asked.

"Your singing, dummy," Kyle said.

"Oh, that," Aleecia said. "Look, I gotta go home. I'm not supposed to see you for a month."

"Your mom's not home," Kyle said.

"No, but I need her to trust me again," Aleecia said. "As if that were possible."

"Well, can I at least give you a ride home after work?" Kyle asked. "Tomorrow night?"

"Um, I guess that would be okay." Aleecia said. "As long as she doesn't see you."

"Kiss me," Kyle said.

"We can't let anyone see us together," Aleecia said. She squeezed his hand and walked toward the bike stand.

//

Aleecia clocked out at eight on Monday and wheeled her bike around to the front parking lot. There were a few cars in the lot, but Kyle flashed his lights so she could find him. She was flooded with feelings as she walked toward his car. *Is this what it feels like to have a boyfriend?* she thought. *I want to be with him but I feel so guilty. My mom was right; I am too young to be having sex. It's too complicated. And besides, it hurts.*

Kyle jumped out of the car to load her bike into the trunk.

"Hi, sweetie." Kyle tried to embrace Aleecia, but she pulled back.

"What's wrong?" Kyle asked after they had gotten in the car.

"I don't know," Aleecia said. "I think this all happened too fast."

"But I love you," Kyle said. "You don't need to worry. I'm here. Forever."

"Forever?" Aleecia asked.

"Yes," Kyle said, squeezing her hand. "Forever."

Aleecia tried to enjoy the ride home—the salty, cool breeze; his hand was so soft, cradling hers. But the guilt was nagging at her. She knew she wasn't supposed to be in Kyle's car. She had never lied to her mother before and now she seemed to by lying all the time.

A couple of blocks from her house, she said, "Stop here. Let me out."

"Sure, honey," Kyle said. He lifted her bike out of the trunk and set it on the street.

"You feel safe, riding home from here?" Kyle asked.

"Yes," Aleecia said. She stood on tiptoe to kiss him. "Everything is okay."

Aleecia pedaled home, not at all sure that anything was okay. *How can I continue sneaking around behind my mother's back?* she thought. *I know she will be able to read the guilt on my face.*

///

The next night and every night after that, Kyle parked in the store lot and waited for Aleecia. They drove to her house in guilty silence, her hand cradled in his, and parked two blocks from her house.

There, they would sit for a few, maybe twenty, minutes, kissing, hugging, and inhaling each other's musk.

One night, after kissing her tenderly, Kyle whispered. "Will you?"

"Will I what?" Aleecia asked.

"Go down on me," Kyle said.

"I don't know how to do that," Aleecia said.

"It's easy," Kyle said, unzipping his pants. "Just like a popsicle."

"I don't know," Aleecia said.

"C'mon, baby," Kyle said. "If you love me."

His penis was hard and it quivered in the light of the street lamp.

Kyle put his hand on the back of Aleecia's neck and pushed her face toward his lap.

Twelve

ALEECIA

ALEECIA GREW INCREASINGLY ANXIOUS, AS HER PERIOD was one week late, and then two. Fearing the worst, she picked up an EPT kit at Big Lots one evening.

"What's in the bag?" Kyle asked as he loaded her bike into his trunk.

"Oh, just some feminine care items, if you must know," Aleecia said. She was annoyed that he had noticed. *Dammit! Why didn't I stuff the bag into my backpack?* she thought.

"Buckle up," Kyle said as he started the car.

They drove in tense silence for a few minutes.

"Is everything okay?" Kyle asked.

Aleecia assumed he was still referring to the items in her bag. "I'm late," she said.

"Late for what?" Kyle asked.

"*Late!*" Aleecia said. "My period."

"Oh my God," Kyle said. "Are you sure? Did you take a test?"

"I bought a test," Aleecia said. "That is what's in the bag. I'll take the test in the morning."

"Text me right away," Kyle said. "Okay?"

"I don't understand," Aleecia said, starting to cry. "We used a condom, didn't we?"

"Well, actually," Kyle said, slowly. "I meant to tell you."

"Tell me what?" Aleecia asked.

"Um—the first one broke," Kyle said.

"Broke?" Aleecia cried.

"It kind of fell apart when I took it off," Kyle said.

"Why didn't you tell me?" Aleecia said. "I could have taken the morning-after pill."

"We fell asleep," Kyle said. "I forgot. I'm sorry, baby. Maybe the test will be negative. Let's hope for the best. Text me tomorrow—as soon as you know for sure."

Kyle pulled over at their usual spot and took Aleecia in his arms.

"Don't worry, Aleecia," Kyle said. "Everything will be okay. I love you."

"I love you too," she said. She felt better, having told him. But she was terrified to face her mother.

//

Aleecia couldn't sleep that night; terrible dreams kept waking her up. In one dream, she was trying to ride her bike up a steep ravine and for some reason she was carrying a bunny in her arms. She had to decide whether to abandon the bike or the bunny in order to make her way to the top. She ended up dropping both the bike and the bunny as she clawed her way out.

Aleecia woke up before her alarm went off and went into the bathroom with her EPT kit. She stared at her reflection for a long time before she unwrapped the stick. *Please God*, she mouthed into the mirror. *Please let the test be negative.* She followed the instructions very carefully, then she set the test stick on the vanity and waited for what she thought was two minutes. There it was—the plus sign. She ripped open the second stick and peed on it. It seemed like mere seconds had passed before the plus sign appeared.

She knew she wasn't ready to tell her mother; she wanted to talk it over with Kyle first.

She wrapped up the sticks in toilet paper and stuffed them into the trash. In disbelief, she stepped into the shower and stood for a long time, letting the hot water spill down her back to rinse away the terrors of the night.

"Bye!" her mom called out from the living room.

Aleecia waited until she heard her mom's car pulling out of the driveway before she texted Kyle.

I'm **pregnant**, she texted.

Are you sure? Kyle texted back.

I took it two times.

See you at lunch? he texted.

Let's not talk about it at school, she replied.

After practice?

I have to work.

After work?

OK, she agreed.

This is it, then, Aleecia thought. *This is really happening.* She had already googled it; the closest abortion clinic was in Orlando, one hundred and twenty miles away. For a minute, she had fantasized that she could get an abortion and not even tell her mother, but she had googled that too. Girls under eighteen had to be accompanied by a parent. *Shit! How can I face my mom? She will never forgive me!*

The day passed in a fog. Aleecia went through the motions, but she couldn't engage with Dawn and Joyce. Their mindless chatter about *American Idol* and Taylor Swift seemed completely irrelevant. The afternoon classes dragged on until, finally, the bell rang and she was able to escape on her bike, pedaling as fast as she could, riding through stop signs and red lights, until she reached Big Lots.

After her shift, Kyle was waiting in the parking lot. He got out of the car as Aleecia approached with her bike. But instead of popping the trunk, he took her into his arms and her bike went crashing to the asphalt. The dream from last night popped back into her head—the bunny and the sound her bike had made when it slipped from her hand.

"Oh, baby," Kyle crooned. He stroked her head as he held her tight.

Aleecia felt numb. She pulled away and climbed into the car while he loaded her bike into the trunk.

//

"You're quiet," Kyle said. He was driving slower than usual. He pulled into the beach parking lot. "Talk to me. What are you thinking?"

"I think my mother is going to kill me," Aleecia

said. "I lied to her and she's never going to forgive me." Aleecia started to cry.

Kyle pulled her to him. "What about the baby?"

"The closest abortion clinic is in Orlando," Aleecia said. "It's going to cost four hundred dollars. And my mom has to go with me."

"Abortion?" Kyle said. "I don't want you to get an abortion."

"What?" Aleecia cried. She pulled away from him. Her cheeks were wet. "What are you saying?"

"I love you, Aleecia," Kyle said. "This is my baby—our baby. I never knew my father. You never knew yours. I want to marry you and be my baby's daddy."

Aleecia had never considered that option—becoming a mother at sixteen, just like her mother had? She was torn. What would be worse—dragging her mother to the abortion clinic and dealing with the humiliation, or living for the rest of her life in the shadow of her mother's disappointment?

After Kyle had dropped her off, Aleecia pedaled

the last few blocks home slowly, pondering her situation. Her brain felt heavy—it was all too much information.

//

She parked her bike in the driveway and opened the screen door.

"Mommy?" she called.

"In here, Aleecia," her mother called from the kitchen.

"I need to tell you something," Aleecia said as she entered the kitchen.

"What, that you're pregnant?" her mother said.

Aleecia gasped.

"I found the sticks in the trash," her mother said.

Thirteen

KYLE

KYLE DROVE TO BIG LOTS EVERY NIGHT AT EIGHT. IT was the only time he could be alone with Aleecia. He was always excited to see her emerge from the back lot, wheeling her beat-up bike. He was planning to surprise her with a new bike for her sixteenth birthday.

"Hey, baby," Kyle said. "I missed you."

Aleecia didn't say anything. She stood sullenly by the car, waiting for him to pop the trunk. She still hadn't said anything as he pulled out of the lot.

"Is everything okay?" Kyle asked.

"I'm late," Aleecia said.

"Are you saying what I think you're saying?" Kyle asked.

"That I could be pregnant?" Aleecia asked. "*Yes!*"

Kyle felt nauseous. He pulled over to the side of the road and tried to breathe. *Fuck me, fuck me, fuck me,* he thought. The memory of that night blasted into his head like a lightning bolt. *When I went to remove the condom, it disintegrated in my hand. She had already fallen asleep beside me. I meant to tell her in the morning but we were in such a rush to get home before her mother woke up. And then there was the whole scene with her mother in the driveway. That's no excuse, I know. It's magical thinking—wishing and hoping—and dreading this moment.*

"I bought a test," Aleecia said. "I'll take it in the morning."

"So maybe you're not pregnant?" Kyle asked. He was flooded with relief.

"I'll find out in the morning," Aleecia said.

"Okay," he said, squeezing her hand. "Text me as soon as you know for sure."

"I don't understand," Aleecia said, starting to cry. "We used a condom."

"Well, actually," Kyle said, slowly. "I meant to tell you—the first one broke."

"Broke?" Aleecia cried.

"It kind of fell apart when I took it off," Kyle said.

"Why didn't you tell me?" Aleecia said. "I could have taken the morning-after pill."

"We fell asleep," Kyle said. "I forgot. I'm sorry, baby. Maybe the test will be negative. Text me tomorrow."

///

The next morning, Kyle lay in bed staring at the ceiling, waiting for his phone to buzz. *C'mon,* he thought. *What is she waiting for? Text me!*

Finally, at six twelve, the phone buzzed and he was afraid to look at it. He lay there with his phone pressed against his chest. *Please God, please God, please God*, he thought. He opened one eye and squinted at the screen.

I'm pregnant, the text read.

Thoughts spun through Kyle's head like a fantasy light show. *College recruiters, NFL draft, the house in Atlanta that I would buy for Dwayne and Crystal—it was all a pipe dream. My mother was right—I will never amount to anything.* But when she was pregnant—first with Dwayne and then with Crystal, the sons of bitches had come around for a while and then disappeared. *That is not going to happen to my Aleecia.*

He couldn't wait to see her again.

///

Kyle picked Aleecia up after work and drove to their usual spot. He pulled over and took her into his arms.

"Don't worry, Aleecia," Kyle said. "Everything will be okay. I love you."

"What do you mean?" she asked. "What are you saying?"

"We had a dream—remember?" Kyle said. "Move to Atlanta, get an apartment big enough for all of us? You, me, the baby, and Dwayne? We can still do this. Don't you want to be a family?"

"I thought it was Nashville," Aleecia said with a wan smile. "My mom, you, me and the baby."

"And Dwayne," Kyle added.

"Yes, and Dwayne," Aleecia said. "But I'm fifteen and you're just starting college. The baby will be four and Dwayne will be twelve by then. What do I do in the meantime?"

"Believe in me," Kyle said. "Wait for me."

"I don't think my mom is on board with that," Aleecia said. "She's taking me to the abortion clinic in Orlando on Saturday."

"Is that what you want?" Kyle asked.

"I don't know what I want," Aleecia said sadly.

//

On Saturday, Kyle woke early and stared at the ceiling. The acrid odor of Dwayne's bunk wafted upward. *Fuck,* he thought, *I'll have to do the laundry before Mom gets up.* Where was Aleecia at this moment? What was she doing? His thoughts ran wild. *What if we ran away together? To Nashville, wherever?*

And then he thought about Dwayne and baby Crystal. *I can never abandon them. What would happen to them if I left? Would Aleecia take them in?* Could they be a family of five together? *Shit, I keep forgetting that she is only fifteen, going on sixteen.* She couldn't, she wouldn't take on all these kids. Why should she?

From the minute he had met her, Kyle saw Aleecia as his salvation, a life raft for him to cling to. *Her faith and the strength that springs from that—that is what I am yearning for. She seems certain about everything and I want to believe in her. She makes me believe in myself. When I am with her, all my dreams seem attainable. I can't imagine living without her, but I never intended to hold her back, or stand in the way of her dreams. A* wave of guilt flooded over him as he thought about the baby. *This isn't right. Aleecia is too young to make a commitment like this. She needs to let it go; I need to let her go.*

Kyle climbed down from his bunk and started to gather up the piles of dirty clothes. Dwayne's eyes were open and watching him.

"Hey, Dwayne," Kyle said. "Help me with the laundry. Get your sheets."

Dwayne gathered up his sheets and followed Kyle into the kitchen and dropped everything on the floor by the washer.

"Let's get you into the bath," Kyle said. He peeled off Dwayne's soiled pajamas and dropped them into the washer.

While Dwayne soaked in the tub, Kyle peeked into his mother's room. Her bed was empty, and Crystal was sitting in her crib wide-eyed.

"Hey, baby," Kyle cooed as he picked her up. "Where's your mama? Are you hungry?" Kyle gathered up her blankets in his spare hand and carted his load to the kitchen.

Kyle cuddled Crystal in his lap as he fed her. Dwayne came padding into the kitchen wrapped in a towel.

"I can't find any clean clothes," Dwayne said.

"I know," Kyle said. "Everything is in the wash. Eat some cereal."

As he watched the kids eating, Kyle thought: *this is what our life could be like. Aleecia will get the kids up in the morning and make everyone breakfast.* He thought about calling her but then he remembered that she was driving to Orlando with her mom. *Not a good time.*

Fourteen

ALEECIA

On Saturday, Aleecia woke up early and washed her hair. While her mother was still asleep, Aleecia sat at the kitchen table with her phone. She opened up the Facebook app and checked out Dawn and Joyce's photos taken at the beach party the night before. Aleecia still had not told them about being pregnant. Gazing at the photos, she felt a million miles removed from the life of a freshman girl. She thought back to the night when Kyle came into Big Lots and invited her to the barbecue. Everything had happened so fast. And now she felt torn between her mom wanting her to get an abortion and Kyle wanting her to keep the baby. *What do I want? I'm not sure!*

Out of curiosity, Aleecia searched on Facebook for teen moms and found a page called Nine Months. She scrolled through the feed and was surprised and comforted to see so many girls voicing her thoughts. Luciana was fourteen and wasn't sure who the father was. Jasmine was a nineteen-year-old college freshman from New Jersey. Shawna and Isabella were both eighteen and their baby daddies were planning to marry them.

Aleecia: My baby-daddy says he'll marry me but my mom wants me to get an abortion. She's taking me to Orlando today.

Luciana: What's in Orlando?

Aleecia: That's the closest abortion clinic. It's 100 miles.

Shawna: Don't do it. Do you love your baby-daddy?

Aleecia: I think so.

Isabella: You need to be sure. This is your life we're talking about.

Shawna: And your baby's life. Have you seen this video? Nick Cannon's "Can I Live"

Luciana: Let us know what happens in Orlando.

Aleecia heard her mom walk into the bathroom and shut the door. She sent friend requests to all the girls who had posted comments so she could follow them.

///

Aleecia tuned the car radio to the gospel station and noticed that her mother's jaw was working; it appeared as though she were arguing with herself without letting the words escape her mouth.

"Mama?" Aleecia asked. "Have you seen this video on YouTube? It's about a baby that wasn't aborted and grew up to be a singer."

"What are you talking about?" her mother asked, distracted.

"I mean, what if my baby grew up to be a famous singer?" Aleecia asked.

"And your point is?" her mother asked.

"I don't think I should have an abortion," Aleecia said.

"Aleecia, we've talked about this," her mother said. "How are you going to feed a baby, much less pay for voice lessons? You need to be realistic."

"But, Mama, you and me, we've always been fine," Aleecia said. "What makes you think I couldn't do as good a job as you?"

Her mother shot her a look out of the corner of her eye. "Nice try, girl. Flattery will get you nowhere." And then she smiled for the first time in days.

"Let's just talk to the doctor and discuss your options. Then we can decide. Okay?"

//

There was a crowd outside the clinic, singing hymns and holding signs. One read, "Women *Do* Regret

Abortion" and another had a graphic image of a bloody fetus.

"Do not look at them," her mother said. "Don't make eye contact. Keep your head down and hold onto my hand."

"Please don't kill your baby!" A woman jumped in front of Aleecia, blocking her path. "You can celebrate a birthday next year!"

"Aleecia, c'mon." Her mother tugged at her hand. She dragged Aleecia into the clinic and slammed the door behind them.

"Mama, please," Aleecia said. "I don't think I can do this."

A nurse approached them. Aleecia read her name tag: Carlotta.

"Can I help you?" Carlotta asked.

"We have an appointment," Aleecia's mother said. "Last name Rivera."

Carlotta checked her clipboard. "Yes, Dr. Mark will be with you in a few minutes." Carlotta looked at

Aleecia's mother and then back at Aleecia. "Aleecia, maybe your mother could wait out here?"

"Okay," Aleecia said.

Aleecia followed Nurse Carlotta into the exam room.

Nurse Carlotta closed the door quietly and turned to Aleecia.

"You seem upset," Nurse Carlotta said.

"I don't know what to do," Aleecia said. "My mother wants me to get an abortion, but Kyle doesn't want me to."

"Kyle is the father?" Nurse Carlotta asked.

"Yes," Aleecia said. She was miserable.

Nurse Carlotta rubbed Aleecia's shoulder. "Aleecia, what do you want? This is your life. You can't let other people decide for you. Abortion isn't your only option. There are a lot of couples that can't have children who would love to adopt your baby."

"Do I have to decide today?" Aleecia asked.

"Let's have Dr. Mark do the exam," Nurse

Carlotta said. "And then we'll talk about your options."

Aleecia sat shivering in a paper gown on the exam table as Dr. Mark finished the exam and left the room.

Nurse Carlotta put her hand on Aleecia's shoulder. "Are you okay, sweetie? Why don't you get dressed and I'll go get your mother."

"Wait," Aleecia said.

Nurse Carlotta hesitated at the door.

"The doctor said I'm four weeks pregnant," Aleecia said. "When do I need to decide?"

"Abortion is legal up to twenty-four weeks," Nurse Carlotta said. "You have some time. But if you choose to abort, the sooner the better, for your own health."

"What do we tell my mother?" Aleecia asked.

"Tell her you need more time," Nurse Carlotta said. "Nobody can force you to choose."

//

Aleecia was quiet on the drive home.

"I made an appointment for next Tuesday," her mother said. "I'll have to take a day off work."

Aleecia didn't say anything.

"Did you hear me?" her mother said. "You'll need to skip school that day."

"I haven't decided, Mama," Aleecia said.

"What do you mean, you haven't decided?" her mother asked.

"I need to talk to Kyle," Aleecia said.

"This is not his decision," Aleecia's mother said.

"No," Aleecia said. "It's mine."

"And mine," her mother said.

"Are you saying you would kick me out of the house?" Aleecia asked.

"No," her mother said. "I would never do that."

They drove for a few miles.

"I tried so hard to be a good mother, to raise you right, so you could have all the things I never did," her mother said.

"I know, Mama," Aleecia said. "You have always

been there for me. This is not your fault. I screwed up. And I am so sorry that I let you down. I just don't think my baby should have to pay for my mistake."

They drove in silence for a few more miles and then her mother spoke.

"We're keeping it, aren't we?"

"Yes, Mama," Aleecia said.

Aleecia sat back and smiled inwardly. Her palms rested light on her belly, suddenly sure in her decision.

Fifteen

KYLE

THE SOUND OF HIS MOTHER'S CAR IN THE DRIVEWAY made the hairs on the back of his neck stand up. *I wish she would go away and never come home again. I wish she were dead. Then Aleecia could move in with us and take care of the kids.*

The screen door slammed. "Where is everyone?" she yelled.

"In the kitchen, Mama," Dwayne yelled back.

"Well look at this," she said as stood at the kitchen door. Kyle stood with his back to her, folding clothes as he pulled them from the dryer.

"Wash my sheets too," she said to Kyle. "And then run to the market for me."

Kyle turned around and glared at her.

"Where have you been?" he said. "Why aren't *you* here making breakfast, doing the laundry and the shopping? Why do I have to do everything?"

"Don't you speak to me like that!" she said. "Maybe if your no-good father had stuck around, you would have more respect."

She pushed past him to pour herself a cup of coffee.

Kyle seethed and he couldn't help himself.

"I'm not going to be around much longer," Kyle said. "I'm moving out."

"Where do you think you're going?"

Kyle felt Dwayne and Crystal staring at him.

"I don't know—maybe move in with Aleecia," he said.

"That little cunt?" his mother said.

"Don't call her that," Kyle said, disgusted. "She's my baby-mama."

"Oh, Christ!" his mother said. "You knocked her up?"

"We're having a baby, yes," Kyle said.

"That's fine," his mother said. "You need to get out of my house anyway, now that you're eighteen and done with school."

"You're throwing me out?" Kyle said. "Who'll take care of the kids when you're out carousing?"

"Dwayne's old enough to look after Crystal," she said.

"He's eight years old, for Christ's sake!" Kyle shouted.

"I was eight when my mama left, and I had to look after my sister," she said.

"Yeah, and where is she now?" Kyle yelled. "Turning tricks in Opa-Locka?"

She turned and slapped him across the face. The blow brought tears to his eyes.

Crystal started to bawl.

"Mama, stop!" Dwayne was crying too. "I don't want to go back to the foster home."

Kyle felt like his head was about to explode. He grabbed his keys and ran out to his car. He needed to get away. He jammed the gear into reverse and peeled out of the driveway and almost sideswiped his mother's car.

He drove fast down Route 1. Rather than risk a speeding ticket, he parked at the beach and ran along the hard sand at the surf line. He ran until he could run no further and then he collapsed on the sand and held his head in his hands, staring out at the ocean, waiting for his heart to slow. Sweat and tears stung his cheeks.

Everything felt overwhelming. *How am I supposed to save Dwayne and Crystal? FSU has offered me a full scholarship to play for the Seminoles. If I made the NFL draft, I'd have enough money to rescue them. But that would take years. And if I went to school in Tallahassee, what would happen to them? And what about Aleecia and the baby?* He imagined piling them all into his car and arriving in Tallahassee to start a new life together. It seemed like the only solution.

When he got back to the house, it was late afternoon. Dwayne was in the living room, playing video games. His mother and Crystal were in the kitchen. She stood over the stove, stirring a pot.

"You went to the market?" Kyle asked.

"Yes, and I finished the laundry and Dwayne made the beds," she said. "You see, we don't need you. You can run off with your little whore and we'll be just fine."

"So we're really doing this?" Kyle asked.

"Jared's moving in," she said. "And he doesn't want you living here anymore."

"Jared? Crystal's daddy?" Kyle asked. "That's where you've been hanging?"

"Yes," she said. "He would have moved in sooner, but he wanted you out of here."

"That asshole!" Kyle said.

"Watch it!" she said. "He's been giving us money."

"What about Dwayne?" Kyle asked. "Doesn't Jared want him gone too?"

"Dwayne's okay for now," she said. "If it becomes a problem, I'll let you know."

"You won't let him hurt Dwayne?" Kyle said. "You'll call me first?"

"I said I would," she said.

Aleecia

Aleecia woke up early on Sunday and logged into Facebook.

Aleecia: My momma said I can keep the baby.

Luciana: Did you go to Orlando?

Aleecia: Yeah, we drove up yesterday. There were protesters and everything.

Candy: I told my parents!

Isabella: And? Girl, don't keep us in suspense!

Candy: My mother is going to call her gyno to schedule an abortion.

Aleecia: They can't make you do that!

Candy: I know. But how am I supposed to have a baby and go to college?

Jasmine: People do it.

Aleecia: Kyle is going to college. We'll be OK.

Aleecia's phone buzzed. Kyle was texting her.

See you at church?

She texted him a smiley face.

///

After church, they found each other among the throng in the parking lot.

"My mom changed her mind," Aleecia said. "She said I don't have to get an abortion."

"Wow," Kyle said. "How did that happen?"

"I reminded her that she kept me," Aleecia said.

"I'm glad she did." Kyle kissed her and took her hand. "I have some news for you too," he said. "Can we go for a walk on the beach?"

"Sure," she said. "My mom said I'm not grounded anymore—now that I'm already pregnant!"

Kyle chuckled.

They drove to the beach and sat in the car staring out at the waves.

"My mom is throwing me out," Kyle said.

"What?" Aleecia cried. "Why?"

"I'm eighteen. She'll lose her benefits if I stay there," Kyle said.

"Where will you go?" she asked.

"You mean where will we go?" he said. He put his arm around her and rested his left hand on her abdomen.

"Let's talk to my mom," Aleecia said. "Maybe you can stay with us."

Aleecia pulled out her phone and texted her mom.

Kyle wants to come over

Her mom replied, Invite him to dinner.

Aleecia grinned. "She said you can come for dinner. Yay!"

"Yay," Kyle whispered into her hair.

Sixteen

ALEECIA

KYLE ARRIVED AT ALEECIA'S HOUSE AT SIX, WEARING black Levi's and a crisp white shirt.

"You dressed up!" Aleecia exclaimed.

"I need your mom to like me," Kyle said. "We should have done this a long time ago."

"Hello, Kyle." Aleecia's mother stood in the kitchen doorway with a platter of chicken.

"Can I help?" Aleecia said. She took the platter from her mother and set it on the table. "Sit down, Mom, we'll get the food."

"Hello, Ms. Rivera," Kyle said. He stood in the

middle of the room, shifting his weight from foot to foot.

"Kyle, come help," Aleecia called from the kitchen.

Aleecia handed him bowls of potatoes and vegetables and she carried the salad.

Once they were all seated and served, Aleecia said grace.

After a few bites, Aleecia's mother put down her fork.

"So, Kyle, what are your plans?" she asked.

Kyle swallowed. "Delicious chicken, ma'am."

"Um, Mom," Aleecia said. "Kyle needs a place to live. Just until school starts."

"Oh?" her mom asked.

"I have a scholarship at FSU," Kyle said. "But I can't live with my mom anymore, now that I'm eighteen."

"Do you have a job?" asked her mother.

"I'm working with my friend, Steve, in construction again this summer," Kyle said.

"Could Kyle stay here with us?" Aleecia asked. "Please?"

"I don't see how," her mother said. "There isn't room."

"What if we finished the garage?" Aleecia asked. "Kyle could do the work, right? There's a toilet out there already."

"Sure, Steve could help," Kyle said. "We could put in dry wall and a subfloor, maybe an outdoor shower?"

"It would be like a little guest house out back," Aleecia said. "I'll work extra hours at Big Lots, and I can use my employee discount to buy everything. Please?"

Her mother sighed. "You can stay on the couch tonight," she said. "Tomorrow, you two need to clean out that garage. Have you looked in there, lately?"

//

The next day, Aleecia knocked on Mr. Martin's door.

"Can I get more hours?" she asked. "Full-time if possible?"

"Are you looking for benefits?" Mr. Martin asked.

"No, I'm on my mom's plan," Aleecia said. "I just need to make more money this summer. We're doing a little remodeling at home."

Mr. Martin rifled through some papers on his desk. "Can you get here by seven?" he said without looking up. "I can give you the opening shift, Monday-Friday, seven to three. That work?"

"That would be awesome!" Aleecia gushed. "Kyle is going to come by this evening to pick up an airbed and some plumbing stuff. I'm putting it on my card, okay?"

"Sure, whatever," Mr. Martin went back to marking up schedules. "Tomorrow morning at seven, right?"

"Yes, sir," Aleecia said.

Kyle

On Sunday after dinner, Kyle went home to clean out his drawers. Dwayne sat morosely on his bed, watching as Kyle filled black garbage bags with his clothes and shoes.

"Why are you leaving?" Dwayne asked. "Because of the fight?"

"No, buddy," Kyle said. "It's time for me to leave. I'm done with school. I need to be out on my own."

"Where are you going?" Dwayne asked. "Can I come?"

"I'm only moving across town, to Aleecia's," Kyle said. "I'll see you all the time."

Kyle stopped packing, sat down on the bed and put his arm around Dwayne.

"Jared is moving in," Kyle said. "Remember Jared, Mom's ex?"

"I hate Jared," Dwayne said.

"I know," Kyle said. "But, look, Mom needs him and Crystal needs a dad. Try and make it work.

Keep your head down and stay out of his way. And if anything bad happens, anything at all, you call me right away, okay?"

Dwayne wrapped his arms around Kyle's waist and buried his head. "Don't leave me here."

Kyle hugged Dwayne. "Don't cry. It will all be okay. I promise," he said.

"Can I sleep with you tonight?" Dwayne said.

"Sure, move over," Kyle said. "As long as you don't wet the bed. As a matter of fact, why don't you go use the bathroom right now? Then I'll lay with you until you fall asleep."

//

Kyle picked Steve up at five the next morning.

"What's all the crap in the back seat?" Steve asked.

"I'm moving in with Aleecia," Kyle said.

"Shit! For real?" Steve asked.

"Her mom is letting us move into the guest house," Kyle said.

"She has a guest house?" Steve asked.

"Well, not yet," Kyle said, laughing. "We need to build it, you and me."

"We're building a house?" Steve said. "We don't have the license to do that."

"We're not building a house, dummy," Kyle said. "We need to finish the garage. The plumbing and electrical are already in there. We need to put in the walls and drop ceiling, sub-floor—the usual shit. We could knock it out in a weekend."

"Two weekends, maybe," Steve said.

"Two, three, whatever," Kyle said. "Are you in?"

"Can we stop at Starbucks?" Steve said.

//

Kyle parked at the address they were given by Mikey, the general contractor.

"What are we building?" Kyle asked.

"We're converting a mini-mall into a health clinic," Mikey said. "You'll be busy all summer."

"Awesome," Steve said.

//

Kyle dropped Steve at his house at four and drove to Big Lots. He dug through the bags in the back seat to find a clean shirt and changed in the car.

Aleecia was working on checkout nine. They had already agreed with Aleecia's mom on a plan. He would sleep in the garage during the construction. The first priority was to build the outdoor shower and replace the utility basin with a vanity so he wouldn't have to share the bathroom in the main house. Kyle filled his cart in the plumbing and carpentry aisles. Then he threw in an airbed and some sheets, pillows and comforter and wheeled his way to aisle nine.

"Mr. Martin gave me a full-time schedule," Aleecia said as she scanned his items. "I'm working seven to three, Monday through Friday."

"You'll have weekends off?" Kyle asked. "You can help with the painting."

"How long do you think before we can move in?" Aleecia asked.

"I'm moving in tonight," Kyle said. "You can stay at my place."

"You know what I mean," Aleecia said, laughing.

The total came to $324.17. Kyle gulped.

Aleecia scanned her employee ID, which brought it down to $194.50. Without skipping a beat, she swung the keypad around and swiped her debit card.

Seventeen

KYLE

K YLE LOOKED AT ALEECIA. *THIS BEAUTIFUL GIRL*, HE
thought as she rang up the items. *She makes everything possible.* He thought back to the previous weekend when he was plotting to rescue the kids. And now here he was, buying home improvement supplies at Big Lots. How had he gotten here?

Kyle drove to Aleecia's house. Her mom wouldn't be home from work until late. He let himself into the garage.

"Shit!" he said aloud.

The garage was packed to the rafters with all the

stuff that Aleecia had picked up on Craig's list. Her mom wasn't kidding. There was no room to inflate the bed so he started carting stuff out into the yard. *I've been up since four this morning and worked eight hours in the hot sun and now this?* His back was sore; he needed a shower. "Unbelievable," he muttered under his breath. *What is up with the hoarding? I've heard about people like this. It was a sign of mental illness, they said. OCD. Does Aleecia have OCD?* He worked for two hours and then it was time to go pick up Aleecia. He let himself into the house with the spare key and showered off.

He dug some clean jeans and T-shirt out of the garbage bags piled in the garage and jumped in the car.

He waited in the Big Lots parking lot, as always. But this time it was different. This time they were going home together. He thought about Dwayne as he sat under the security light and watched the enormous insects swarm.

He texted his mom, Tell Dwayne to call me
Lucifer responded. He's already asleep
It's early, Kyle texted.

Jared sent him to bed without dinner.

Fuck! Kyle thought. *It's only been one day and it's already started. I need to get Dwayne out of there.*

Tell Dwayne I'm going to pick him up after work tomorrow, around 4.

No response.

//

That night Aleecia and Kyle lay on the airbed in the garage.

"What is all this crap?" Kyle asked.

"I found it on Craigslist," Aleecia said.

"And . . . " Kyle said. "What were you planning to do with it?"

"I guess I'm a bit of a hoarder," Aleecia said.

"Ya think?" Kyle asked. "We need to get rid of everything if we're going to live in here."

"What will we do with it?" Aleecia asked softly. She wasn't ready to let it all go. As she looked around she remembered the adrenaline rush that she had felt with each new discovery. All of the stuff her mom had said she couldn't afford to buy her as a little girl, she had found for free.

"I don't know," Kyle barked. "Call the sanitation department?"

"Is everything alright?" Aleecia asked.

"It's my little brother, Dwayne," Kyle said. "My mom's boyfriend is abusing him."

"Oh my God," Aleecia said. "What do we do?"

"I don't know," Kyle said. "I'm going over there tomorrow after work to see what's going on."

///

The next evening, Kyle arrived at the house at five to find it locked up tight. He tried his key, but it didn't work.

Where r u, he texted his mother. Where is Dwayne?

No response.

You changed the fucking locks? he texted.

No response.

Kyle banged on the front door and living room windows. He walked around to the back and peered into Dwayne's bedroom window. He saw Dwayne curled up at the foot of his bed. He tried to open the window but it was locked. He banged on the window, crying, "Dwayne, wake up!"

Dwayne rolled over and stared with wide eyes. It was as though he didn't recognize Kyle.

"Dwayne!" Kyle yelled. "Open the window!"

Dwayne walked over to the window and tried to open it, but it was nailed shut.

"Can you open the back door?" Kyle yelled.

"I can't," Dwayne shouted back. "They nailed it shut."

"What the fuck?" Kyle took off his T-shirt and wrapped it around his right hand.

"Get away from the window!" he yelled. Kyle swung at the window and punched a hole in the glass. He swung several more punches to knock all the shards loose. He laid the T-shirt on the window frame and reached in to grab Dwayne by the armpits. As he picked him up, Kyle was surprised at how small Dwayne seemed. And shocked at how bad he smelled.

Kyle carried Dwayne to the car and set him down on the seat.

"How long were you locked in there?" Kyle asked.

"Since yesterday," Dwayne said and began to cry. "I don't want to stay here."

"Don't worry, you're never coming back." Kyle said.

//

Aleecia was working a double shift to cover for someone who had called in sick, so Kyle drove straight to Big Lots. On the way, they passed a KFC.

"Can we stop?" Dwayne asked.

"Sure, of course, you must be starving," Kyle said. He pulled up to the drive-through window and ordered a large bucket of Extra Crispy Bites and a large Pepsi.

When they got to Big Lots, Kyle told Dwayne to wait in the car with the A.C. on. Dwayne stuffed a piece of chicken into his mouth and nodded; his face was covered with grease. He was in heaven.

Kyle approached checkout nine and stood at the foot of the conveyor belt while Aleecia finished ringing up a customer—a guy in his early twenties buying power tools. He saw her smiling and blushing. *She's flirting with him!* he thought. When she handed the guy the receipt, it seemed that she hung on to her end a little too long and Kyle flashed back to the first time they met. *Does she do that with every guy?* he wondered.

Aleecia startled when she saw him.

"I need to talk to you," Kyle said.

"Meet me by the men's room," Aleecia said. Kyle took off.

Aleecia paged Mr. Martin on the intercom, and he appeared almost instantly. "I need to use the ladies room," she lied. Mr. Martin knew she was expecting and accommodated her frequent visits to the restroom. Aleecia raced back to the restroom and arrived breathless.

"Now, I really do need to pee," she said. Aleecia

grabbed his arm and pointed at the handicapped restroom. "In here," she said.

"What is it?" Aleecia asked. "What's the emergency? Don't watch me!"

While Aleecia peed, Kyle turned his back to her and related the story of going to the house and finding Dwayne locked in his room—nailed in, in fact.

"Where is he now?" Aleecia asked.

"In the car, stuffing his face with KFC," Kyle said. "He can't go back there, and I can't let the county take him."

"Take him to my house and get him cleaned up," Aleecia said. "We'll talk to my mom when she gets home."

Kyle kissed her. He started to leave and then hesitated. "Hey," he said. "Do you flirt with all of your customers?"

"Really?" Aleecia said, laughing. "That's what you want to ask me right now?"

Eighteen

ALEECIA

STORE TRAFFIC SLOWED DOWN AFTER LUNCH, SO ALEECIA asked Mr. Martin if she could clock out at two. And in truth, she was feeling a little queasy. She was throwing up almost every morning.

Kyle and Steve hadn't yet started on the remodeling project, so they had rigged a curtain around the toilet. Aleecia nagged Kyle about constructing real walls and a real door around the toilet, but he didn't see it as a priority.

"What do you care?" Kyle asked. "You can use the bathroom inside the house."

"Except when it's an emergency!" she reminded him. "And I'm having more and more of those. Besides, do you think I like listening to you relieve yourself in the middle of the night?"

Kyle laughed. "I'll be leaving for Tallahassee in a few weeks. Then you'll miss everything I do in the middle of the night."

"I doubt that," Aleecia said, laughing. But she was keenly aware of the passage of time and that he'd be leaving soon. *I don't want him to leave*, she thought and then realized how selfish that was. She dreaded returning to high school to face the humiliating stares and whispers alone. But she knew that college was the right choice for him, for both of them.

//

Kyle had talked about his little brother and sister all the time, even fantasized about bringing them to come live with them in the garage "guest house." When Kyle told her that Crystal's father was back,

Aleecia thought that everything sounded okay. But when Kyle showed up at Big Lots and told her what had happened, she felt certain that they needed to intervene. She just wasn't sure how, or whether her mom would agree.

When she got to the house, Kyle and Dwayne were in the living room watching TV.

"Hi, boys," Aleecia said.

"Dwayne, this is Aleecia," Kyle said. "You're home early. What time does your mom usually get home?"

"It got slow, so I told Mr. Martin I wasn't feeling well," Aleecia said. "And actually, I'm not."

Kyle jumped up. "Baby, you need to sit down." He led her to the couch. "Do you want some water?"

"Maybe some iced tea," Aleecia said. "Herbal."

Aleecia got up and followed Kyle into the kitchen.

"We can't talk to my mom in front of Dwayne," Aleecia said.

"He's probably exhausted," Kyle said. "I'll settle him in the garage and let him play with my phone."

"Hey, Dwayne," Kyle called out. "Let's brush your teeth."

///

Aleecia was resting on the couch, surfing through channels when she heard her mom's car.

She texted Kyle, mom's here

He replied, b right there.

Her mother came in loaded with grocery bags. Kyle rushed to her side. "Let me get those, Ms. R."

"You're going to have to start calling me Mom," Aleecia's mom laughed. "There's more in the car."

Kyle went to retrieve the groceries.

"Mama, sit down," Aleecia said. "Do you want some tea?"

"There's some wine coolers in the fridge," her mother said. "That would be nice." She sank into the easy chair and put her feet up on the ottoman. "Oh, what a day," she started.

"Um, Mama," Aleecia said, handing her mother her drink. "There's something we need to talk about."

Silence.

"I'm listening," her mother said.

Aleecia started to tell the history of Kyle's mother and her boyfriend. Kyle jumped in to relay the events of the day and finished with, "I had to bring him here. He can't go back there."

"We need to call the police," Aleecia's mother said.

"The county will take Dwayne away," Kyle said. "I can't let that happen to him again."

"Dwayne is terrified, Mama," Aleecia said.

"I don't know what you're planning to do," Aleecia's mother said. "Dwayne has a mother. You can't just take him away from her—that's kidnapping. We'll all go to jail."

"Here's an idea," Kyle said. "I'll talk to her in the morning and see if she'll give me custody. Jared really doesn't want Dwayne around. I bet she'll go for it."

"You better call her right now and let her know

where he is," her mother said. "She might have already called the cops."

"Dwayne has my phone," Kyle said and headed for the back door.

Aleecia's mother gave her a hard look. "And if Kyle gets custody, what does that mean for you, for us? You're bringing me another mouth to feed? You're taking on this boy's entire family. Are you ready for this much motherhood?"

"Mama, I don't know." Aleecia started to cry. "I just know it's the right thing to do."

Kyle returned with his phone. "Thank God, Dwayne fell asleep. My mom called five times and sent some pretty nasty texts."

"What did she say?" Aleecia asked.

"You don't want to know," Kyle said.

He texted Lucifer: Dwayne is here with me. I'll call you tomorrow.

Lucifer replied: Not too early. Don't want to wake Jared

"Okay," Aleecia's mother said. "What are the sleeping arrangements?"

"I'll sleep out back with Dwayne," Kyle said to Aleecia. "Okay if you sleep in your room?"

"Sure, but what are we going to do tomorrow?" Aleecia asked. "We both need to work."

"I'll drop him off at my aunt's house on my way to work," Kyle said. He took Aleecia's face in his hands. "I got this, baby. You don't need to worry. I've been managing things at my house for years."

When Kyle had left, Aleecia's mom said, "I have to say, I am impressed with this boy."

"Yeah," Aleecia said. "If only he could get to work on the remodel and build that damn bathroom!"

//

That night, in bed, Aleecia logged onto Facebook.

Aleecia: My baby daddy brought his little brother to come live with us

Isabella: Who is us?

Aleecia: OMG! I forgot to tell you that Kyle moved in with me. We're living in my mom's garage.

Jasmine: You're living in the garage?

Aleecia: Kyle is a carpenter. He's putting in walls and everything. We live in Florida, so it's not like it ever gets that cold

Luciana: So what's with the little brother? How old?

Aleecia: Dwayne is 8. Kyle's mom's boyfriend threw the boys out of the house. Can you believe that?

Shawna: I believe it. My mom wants to throw me out!

Candace: Jesus. And I thought my mom was a bitch!

Nineteen

KYLE

A T NOON THE NEXT DAY, KYLE GOT A TEXT FROM Lucifer: I piled all of Dwayne's shit out front. Come pick it up.

Kyle: WTF? His clothes, his puzzles, his G.I Joes, his PlayStation? You left it all out on the lawn? Somebody might steal it

Lucifer: Well, you'd better rush over here

Kyle: I'll be there at 4.

Fucking cunt, he thought. *What is wrong with her?*

///

Kyle's construction crew clocked out at three-thirty and after dropping Steve at home, Kyle drove like a madman, desperately trying to arrive home in time to salvage Dwayne's clothes and toys. He was ecstatic when he pulled into the driveway to see that she had left everything on the porch. He gathered the piles into trash bags and made several trips to the car. When he had finished, he realized that Dwayne's PlayStation was missing.

Kyle pressed his face to the screen door and yelled, "Yo! Anybody home?"

His mother called out, "What do you want?"

"Where is the PlayStation?" Kyle shouted.

His mother walked into the living room and stood several feet inside the door. "Jared wants to keep that," she said. "Crystal may want it someday."

Kyle was furious. "It doesn't belong to Jared," he said. "I bought it for Dwayne for Christmas! It belongs to Dwayne. Give it to me."

"You're going to have to come in and get it," his

mother said. "Jared told me that I can't give it to you. And he said you need to pay to get the window fixed."

"And what about nailing the windows and doors shut? Who's going to pay to repair all that damage?" Kyle fumed. He opened the screen door and pushed past his mother to grab the PlayStation.

"Don't you dare hit me!" she cried.

"What are you talking about? I've never hit you! You're confusing me with Jared. Now get outta my way, bitch!" Kyle yanked the cables from the TV and shoved his way back out the door, dragging the controllers behind him.

"I'll call the cops," his mother yelled.

"Yeah, you do that!" Kyle yelled. "The cops would love to hear how you locked your son in his room without food, water, or a toilet for two days."

//

Kyle peeled out of the driveway; the tires left black rubber tread marks on the road. The veins on his neck and forehead were bulging in anger. He fought to hold back his tears. A few blocks from the house, he pulled over to compose himself. He didn't want Aleecia to see him like this.

Why is my life so fucked? he wondered. *Why did that bitch ever give birth to Dwayne and me?* And then he caught himself. *Why am I pressuring Aleecia to have a baby at fifteen?* She was still just a kid. No matter how hard she might try, she wasn't prepared to be a mother—she had no clue what lay ahead of her—the cost, the responsibility, the complete loss of freedom; she might never get a chance to go to college and certainly would never make it to Nashville. *I need to tell her that it's okay if she decides to abort the baby. This is all wrong and it's all my fault.*

He pulled back onto the highway and started driving slowly toward Aleecia's house. Then he thought, *What about me? She is the best thing that ever happened to me. If she aborted the baby, what would she need me for? I'll be out on the street. In six weeks, I'll be leaving for Tallahassee; better wait until then to tell her any of this. There would still be time if she decides she wanted to abort after all. Besides, her mother knows all of this—it' not my place to tell her that she is too young.*

Kyle was about to turn left onto Aleecia's street when he suddenly remembered.

"Fuck!" Kyle said aloud. "I forgot to pick up Dwayne."

He made a U-turn and drove back across town to his Aunt Georgia's house.

///

Dwayne was waiting on the front porch and raced to the car to greet Kyle.

"You came back!" Dwayne crowed.

"Well, of course I came back," Kyle said. "What did you think, dummy?"

"Aunt Georgia said if you knew what was good for you, you'd run off to Tallahassee and leave all of us behind," Dwayne said.

Kyle was shocked. Georgia had voiced his very

own thoughts? What if he did leave everyone behind? Was that even a possibility? Would Dwayne forgive him if he pursued his football career and promised to come back for him when he had made enough money?

"Not only did I come back," Kyle said. "But look what I brought you!" Kyle gestured toward the back seat.

"My PlayStation!" Dwayne screamed.

"Yeah, and all your other toys and your clothes, too," Kyle said.

Dwayne flung himself into Kyle's arms. "Thank you!"

"Let's go home, Dwayne," Kyle said softly.

//

Kyle tooted the horn, excited to see Aleecia standing in the doorway when he pulled into the driveway. *This is it*, he thought, *this is what home feels like.*

Dwayne jumped out of the car and ran to the house.

"Aleecia, look!" he cried. "Kyle brought all my stuff."

Kyle watched in awe as Aleecia smiled and embraced Dwayne. *She's going to be an amazing mom*, he thought.

"First things first," Kyle said as he reached the porch. "Got to set up the PlayStation. Will your mom mind?'

"I think my mom actually likes having all us around," Aleecia said. "She's always wanted a big family like she grew up in."

Kyle wired the device to the TV and Dwayne settled on the couch with his games. Aleecia retreated to the kitchen to make dinner while Kyle carted all of the stuff from the car out to the garage.

Kyle surveyed the garage and thought, *we really need to tackle this mess*. He made a mental note to finish dumping all of Aleecia's accumulated junk first thing Saturday morning. Priority two was to install the outdoor shower and then install flooring and drywall and build a closet. The place needed so much work that he wondered if they could finish the project before he left for Tallahassee.

//

As the summer wore on, Kyle noticed that Aleecia was slowing down and tiring easily. He often heard her retching in the bathroom while he and Dwayne were eating breakfast. He was worried about her riding her bike home from work every day in the afternoon heat. Kyle dreaded leaving for Tallahassee, but the daily texts kept coming from the freshman football coach with updates on the training schedule. It seemed as though Aleecia was in complete denial about his impending departure. He knew he needed to broach the subject with her but he wasn't sure how or when to do it.

Twenty

ALEECIA

THE SUMMER PASSED QUICKLY. ALEECIA'S MORNINGS were a buzz of activity: wake up at the crack of dawn, reel from morning sickness, make breakfast and pack lunches for Kyle and Dwayne and kiss them both goodbye before collapsing on her bed for another half-hour of sleep. She vaguely remembered her mom leaving for work each morning before her alarm went off at six.

The evenings were altogether different. Aleecia got home first and had time for a quick shower after the sweaty bike ride from Big Lots. Kyle and Dwayne arrived around five and burst through the screen door, boisterous and hungry. Aleecia fed Dwayne and settled him in the garage with his PlayStation while Kyle showered. Aleecia set the table with candles from Pier 1, then dimmed the lights and turned the country station on low to create an atmosphere of serenity for when her mom arrived. Aleecia and Kyle sat with her mom over a leisurely dinner, after which Kyle and Aleecia did the dishes while her mom relaxed in the living room.

"I could get used to this!" her mom called from the living room.

"We want you to," Aleecia called back. She chuckled as she leaned her hip into Kyle, who stood drying dishes beside her.

"Baby, we need to talk," Kyle said.

Aleecia hesitated.

"Now what?" she asked. "Baby Crystal is moving in?"

Kyle stopped drying dishes and turned to face Aleecia. He flung the dishtowel over his shoulder.

"You know I'm leaving, right?" Kyle said. "Preseason practice starts in two weeks. I'm getting the sense that you're in denial about this—telling your mom to get used to the way things are."

"I'm not in denial—I guess I was hoping you'd choose us over football," Aleecia said.

"Baby, it's not football I'm choosing; it's our future," Kyle said. "I need to go to Tallahassee to get drafted into the NFL. I need to do this to take care of you and our baby."

Aleecia was miserable. What he was describing was a far-off dream, years in the future. *What about tomorrow and the next day? How am I supposed to do this alone?*

"Talk to your mama," Kyle said, reading her thoughts. "This is our best shot. She agrees."

"What do you mean she agrees? You talked to my mom?" Aleecia asked. "Without discussing it with me? What am I, a child?"

Aleecia was distraught. She couldn't tell whether this was a real feeling or just a hormonal response.

"I need to lie down," she said and stormed out of the kitchen.

Aleecia locked herself in her room and cried herself to sleep.

In the morning, everyone was gone and Aleecia was bereft. *So this is what it will feel like—to be all alone.*

Aleecia felt listless all day at work. The lines of customers, the beeps and boops of the scanner, the days and weeks and months stretched out in front of her, no sign of joy in sight.

Her mood was gray as she pedaled home that night. She moved slowly through her routine of showering and prepping dinner. Dwayne's loud energy only served to annoy her and she felt like there was a gray cloud of fog between her and the others at dinner that night.

"Are you okay?" Kyle and her mother exchanged worried looks.

"I'm tired," Aleecia said. "I need to lie down." She padded to her room and closed the door.

Kyle started to clear the table.

"Aleecia, honey," her mother said, tapping on the door.

"It's open," Aleecia said.

Aleecia's mother entered and sat on the bed. "What is it, baby?"

"He's leaving, Mama," Aleecia said.

"I know," her mother said. "It's for the best. You kids need to both go to college. This is his shot."

Aleecia was quiet.

Her mother rubbed her back and hummed in a low voice. Aleecia recognized a lullaby from her childhood.

"Mama," Aleecia said. "I don't want to do this alone."

"Do what?" her mother said.

"I think I want to get abortion," Aleecia said.

A long silence.

"Yeah, Kyle won't fight you on that," her mother said.

"You talked to him?" Aleecia was indignant.

Everyone else had a plan for their lives, and they were all talking about her behind her back.

"Why would he say that?" Aleecia demanded. "Is he planning to walk away?"

"No, baby," her mother said. "Just all this mess with Dwayne and his mom and all. Kyle wants a future for you, and doesn't want this baby to be the thing standing in your way."

"I think I need to talk to Kyle," Aleecia said.

"Yes, you do," her mother said. "And baby, you know whatever you decide I'm here for you. You will never be alone."

///

Aleecia marched out to the garage. She pounded on the door and immediately regretted it. Kyle opened the door, wild-eyed.

"Dwayne is sleeping," he whispered.

"Where can we talk?" Aleecia asked.

"I don't know," Kyle said. "Take a drive? Maybe to the beach?"

"Okay," Aleecia said.

They drove in silence for a mile or so.

"Paint me a picture," Aleecia said. "What do the next five years look like?"

"I can't promise anything," Kyle said.

"Oh, that's just great." Aleecia started to cry.

"I can't promise but here's what I want for us," Kyle said. "I'll find a place in Tallahassee for me and Dwayne. We have cousins there. Let's just say they agree to watch Dwayne and get him to school every day. I'll work my ass off to make starter and get drafted. I'll text you every day and I'll come back every chance I get. It's like a six-hour drive."

"You told Mama that I should have an abortion?" Aleecia asked.

"I never said that," Kyle said.

"But that's what you think?" Aleecia said.

"Aleecia, this should never have happened to you," Kyle said. "I love you so much; I think the world of you and I don't want anything I did to stand between you and your dreams."

"This is our baby," Aleecia said.

"Yes, and I love you and it . . . him, her . . . " Kyle said. "But my mom was sixteen, your mom was what, seventeen? What if we didn't do that? What if we were in our twenties? What if I was playing for the NFL and you had a recording contract? What if we had waited?"

"Well, we didn't wait," Aleecia said. "And here we are." She was sobbing.

Kyle pulled over and gathered Aleecia in his arms. "Let's just take it one day at a time. I'll be back at Christmas. Will you be okay? The baby isn't due until March. The season will be over by then."

Aleecia couldn't feel anything anymore.

Twenty-one

KYLE

ALEECIA MADE DINNER FOR THE FOUR OF THEM EVERY night. She always had supper ready for Dwayne as soon as he ran in, famished. Then she'd prepare a nice dinner for Kyle and her mother. She didn't seem to have much of an appetite but she seemed to savor the relaxed dinner conversation. And he knew that Aleecia's mother really appreciated being waited on every night.

One evening as they were washing the dishes, Aleecia's mom said something like, "I could get used to this."

Aleecia's reply shocked Kyle. "We want you to."

I need to say something! "You know I'm leaving in two weeks?" Kyle said.

"I guess I was hoping you'd choose me over football," Aleecia said.

How could she think that was an option? Football was their ticket out of poverty. He couldn't support Aleecia and the baby and Dwayne on a carpenter's paycheck. *And we can't live in the garage forever.* At times like this, he was reminded of how young she was.

"I may not make it to the NFL, but I've got to give it a shot, right? Talk to your mom," Kyle said. "She'll explain it to you."

Aleecia was livid. She stormed out of the kitchen and locked herself in her room.

Kyle exchanged looks with Aleecia's mom.

"Let her sleep," she said. "She'll see things differently in the morning."

But the next night when Kyle arrived home, Aleecia seemed worse, withdrawn and irritable; she was short with Dwayne. He had never seen her like this.

"Are you okay?" her mother asked.

"I'm tired," Aleecia said. "I need to lie down." She locked herself in her room again.

Kyle cleared the table and washed the dishes. Then he went out to the garage where Dwayne was playing video games.

"Time for bed," Kyle said.

"Noooo," Dwayne protested.

"C'mon, we gotta get up at four a.m." Kyle said.

"Why do we always have to wake up so early?" Dwayne whined.

"You know I got to work," Kyle said. "Go use the toilet and brush your teeth."

Kyle fell asleep as soon as his head hit the pillow. The next thing he knew, someone was pounding on the door. Kyle was surprised to see Aleecia standing there, her faced streaked with tears.

"Are you crazy?" Kyle asked. "You'll wake Dwayne!"

"I'm sorry," Aleecia said. "But I need to talk to you—right now!"

"Let's talk in the car," Kyle said. "We don't need to wake up the whole neighborhood."

//

They drove in silence for a mile or so.

"Tell me the truth," Aleecia said. "Are you coming back from Tallahassee?"

"I can't promise anything," Kyle said.

"Oh, that's just great." Aleecia started to cry again.

"Look here's my plan," Kyle said. "I'm taking Dwayne with me to Tallahassee. We have cousins there. They said they'd watch him for me so I can focus on making starter and getting drafted by the NFL. We'll text every day."

"Will you come back on weekends?" Aleecia asked.

"It's a six-hour drive," Kyle said. "I'll come when I can."

He could feel Aleecia glaring at him in the dark.

"I'm sorry, baby," Kyle said. "I'm doing my best."

"You told Mama that you want me to get an abortion?" Aleecia asked.

"She said that?" Kyle asked.

"Pretty much," Aleecia said. "You want to run off to Tallahassee and pretend this whole thing never happened? Where would you be living right now if my mom hadn't offered us the garage?"

"Aleecia, you're getting emotional," Kyle said. "But my mom was sixteen, your mom was what, seventeen? What if we didn't do that? What if we were in our twenties? What if I was playing for the NFL and you had a recording contract? What if we had waited?"

"Well, we didn't wait," Aleecia said. "And here we are." She was sobbing.

Kyle pulled over and gathered Aleecia in his arms. "I'll be back at Christmas," he said. "The baby isn't due until March. The season will be over by then."

"Will you stay with me tonight?" Aleecia asked.

"In your room?" Kyle said. "Okay."

//

Kyle shut the bedroom door very carefully and stood watching Aleecia undress. Her body was full and luscious. He lay down beside her on the bed and pulled her to him. *Everything about this feels wrong. We haven't been together since the night of the prom.* He was overcome with desire and guilt.

//

August passed quickly and soon, it was time to leave. Kyle washed all of his and Dwayne's clothes and folded everything neatly in black garbage bags. Aunt Georgia's stepsister, Louise, had agreed to take Dwayne in after school in exchange for two hundred dollars a week. Kyle was wary but agreed to give it a try.

"How about it?" Kyle asked.

"Who is Cousin Louise?" Dwayne asked.

"She's family," Kyle said. "Don't worry, I'll pick you up after practice every day."

Aleecia stood in the doorway, her arms folded across her chest.

"So this is goodbye?" Aleecia asked.

"Dwayne, take this bag out to the car," Kyle said.

Dwayne grabbed the bag and ran out, humming the tune to Pharrell Williams' "Happy."

"Aleecia, baby," Kyle said. He kissed her. "I'm doing this for us—you need to know that. Be strong."

//

Dwayne needed to stop every hour to use a restroom. He'd see the sign in the distance—a Wendys, a Subway, a Waffle House—and start the chant, "Ooh, ooh, ooh, gotta go!"

At each stop, he'd beseech, "I'm hungry!"

"Seriously, man," Kyle said. "What is wrong with you?"

"I never been anywhere but Fort Pierce my whole life," Dwayne said. "I'm going places!"

"Your whole long life?" Kyle asked. He couldn't help himself. He laughed. "Well, we're heading for the big city now."

With all the stops, the drive was taking a lot longer than Kyle had planned. He looked at his phone. It was already three o'clock. While he waited in the McDonald's parking lot, he texted Aleecia.

Halfway to Tallahassee. R U OK?

Aleecia replied: Dawn's here. I'm OK now.

Kyle felt a flood of relief and love for her. He grinned from ear to ear. *Good girl,* he thought. *You'll make it through.*

He texted a smiley face.

When they finally exited at Tallahassee and saw the first signs for FSU, Kyle said to Dwayne, "I found us a room in a rooming house on Craigslist. Let's check this place out and tomorrow we'll get up early and drop you with Cousin Louise."

Dwayne grunted acceptance.

Twenty-two

ALEECIA

THE TRANSITION BACK TO HIGH SCHOOL LIFE WASN'T AS tough as Aleecia had anticipated. Sure, she knew people were whispering behind her back and she felt their eyes surveying her body for any signs of development. But one benefit of her pregnancy was that she was excused from gym class, which she had always detested. Aleecia spent that period with the other pregos in the assistant dean's office. Ms. Jamison was already plotting a home-study program for the girls so they could stay on track with their studies and graduate on time.

Aleecia looked around the room at the other three girls and smiled to herself, remembering Isabella's comment on Facebook: "You can form a club. An extra-curricular activity you can put on your resume!" The other girls were much farther along—their babies were due around Christmas.

Aleecia raised her hand.

Ms. Jamison nodded at her.

"How long can I stay in school?" Aleecia asked.

"What's your due date?" Ms. Jamison flipped through some papers on her clipboard. "March twentieth? We don't want anybody going into labor on school grounds so we usually send girls home a month before their due date." Ms. Jamison looked up. "Depending on what your doctor says, you can probably stay until spring break. You'll home-school for the balance of your sophomore year and you might be able to take your final exams in class with your peers. Sound good?"

"Now girls," Ms. Jamison addressed the group. "In order to stay in this program, you must have monthly checkups with your doctors and have them fill out a health form each time. Healthy mommies, healthy babies."

The girls giggled.

///

Aleecia was eager to get back to singing and arrived early at rehearsal on Thursday night. Something was wrong. Instead of the excited reception she was expecting, everyone seemed standoffish.

Mr. Buckles approached her. "Aleecia, we weren't expecting you."

"What?" asked Aleecia. "Why not?"

Mr. Buckles took her by the arm and pulled her to the side of the room. "Aleecia, we can't allow girls in your condition to sing in front of the congregation. This is the Lord's house."

"Oh!" Aleecia cried. She was overcome with shame and confusion.

"Look," Mr. Buckles said, "Father Rick has just joined us as associate pastor. Why don't you schedule a counseling session with him? He can help guide your soul in the path the Lord has chosen for you."

Aleecia turned and walked out of the church slowly, deliberately feigning calm resolve. Her face burned with humiliation but she didn't want the others to know.

When she got home she logged onto Facebook. Her feed included selfies from the other girls in various stages of pregnancy.

Aleecia: I got thrown out of the church choir. Apparently pregnant girls aren't fit to sing the Lord's praises.

Candy: Hypocritical bastards!

Aleecia: I'm supposed to go for pastoral counseling with Father Rick

Jasmine: Who is that?

Aleecia: He's a new junior minister. Just moved here from California. I heard he is really hot

Luciana: Hot? This could get interesting! Post photos

Aleecia's phone buzzed. Kyle was texting her.

Kyle: How was rehearsal?

Aleecia: They kicked me out. I gotta go for pastoral counseling

Kyle: That's bullshit!

Aleecia: How is football practice?

Kyle: Awesome. I'm starting running back. Big game this weekend

Aleecia: When are you coming to visit?

Kyle: Don't know baby. But Dwayne says hi

///

On Saturday, Aleecia knocked tentatively on Father Rick's door. No answer. She rapped a little louder. The door swung open. Father Rick was in his late twenties with broad shoulders, a full head of curly black hair, and a graceful Roman nose.

"You must be Aleecia," Father Rick said. "Come in."

Once they were seated, Father Rick began. "Everything you tell me in here is confidential. Nobody will ever know, not even your mother. Feel free to tell me everything that is going on with you."

Aleecia relayed the whole story—prom night, the broken condom, Kyle moving into her garage and fixing it up. Father Rick was silent, letting her keep talking as she went on about Dwayne coming to stay and then both of them leaving for Tallahassee, the home-school program for pregnant teens, and then getting kicked out of the choir.

When she finished, they sat in silence for a moment.

"How old are you, Aleecia?" Father Rick asked.

"Sixteen," Aleecia said.

"Do you accept Jesus as your savior?" Father Rick asked.

"I do," Aleecia said.

"That's good," Father Rick said. "Take my hand."

His hand was soft and warm. Aleecia's nerves were on fire with a tingling sensation that pulsated throughout her body.

"Let's pray together," Father Rick said.

Aleecia didn't hear his words; she felt the vibration of his intonation and her body rocked rhythmically in time with his.

When he was done, Father Rick embraced Aleecia and she inhaled his spicy aftershave. Father Rick released her and held her at arm's length.

"Aleecia, I want to help you to find the Lord," Father Rick said. "The Lord can save you."

Aleecia wasn't sure what she was being saved from, but she wanted to see Father Rick again. "Yes," she said.

"Can you meet after school?" Father Rick asked.

Aleecia's heart raced. "Sure," she said. "What time?"

"Let's meet at four every day," Father Rick said. "Does that work?"

"I have to work on Mondays, Wednesdays and Saturdays," Aleecia said.

Father Rick consulted his calendar. "What if we meet Tuesday, Thursday and Friday at four? And then, I'll see you after church on Sunday. I'm leading the youth group on Sunday after service. Will you join?"

Aleecia was willing to do whatever Father Rick asked of her. *I have always loved the church—it means everything to me.* Maybe God could forgive her. Maybe she could find meaning in her choice to have Kyle's baby.

Twenty-three

ALEECIA

ALEECIA BEGAN PRAYING WITH FATHER RICK THREE TIMES a week. Prayer gave her life some resonance. As an added benefit, she wasn't missing Kyle anymore. She'd hear about his accomplishments in the halls at school—his forty-, sixty-, or eighty-yard runs for touchdowns—and the Seminoles' undefeated season. But she didn't think about him often, didn't wait with bated breath for him to text her. Aleecia was finding in her relationship with Father Rick a sense of purpose and belonging. Motherhood was her calling; music could wait. Between prayer sessions, she found solace in the Bible.

Kyle had started out the semester by texting her every day about his classes, his practices, and how well Dwayne was doing. She'd respond with a Bible verse and a smiley face. Then his texts started appearing less frequently—four, then three, then one a week.

"How is Kyle doing at school?" her mother asked her one night over dinner.

"Good, I think," Aleecia said.

"You think?" her mother probed. "You mean you don't know?"

"I'm not paying too much attention," Aleecia said. "I think the team is winning but Kyle isn't a starting player. Something like that."

"Don't you think you should show a little more interest?" her mother asked. She sounded worried.

"I'll tell you what I'm interested in," Aleecia said, emphatically. "And it's not football! My Bible lessons with Father Rick are much more interesting than football. Father Rick is so wonderful! The way he holds my hand in prayer circle and the way he listens to me when I'm talking. I think he loves me."

"Aleecia," her mother said slowly. "Could you be imagining these feelings for Father Rick? He's a grown man. He can't possibly have these feelings for you."

"You just don't know, mom."

"Changing the subject—what does the doctor say about the baby? How is your health?" her mother asked.

"Well, it's kinda obvious, isn't it mom?" Aleecia said, exasperated. "I look like a beached whale. Dr. Janec thinks I'm putting on too much weight. But I don't eat anything, I don't understand."

"What about all the ice cream?" her mother asked. "You must go through a quart every night."

"Mom! I like to eat ice cream when I'm in the tub. And it's full of calcium—is that so bad?"

///

As her belly began to swell and her emotional state became more volatile, Aleecia imagined a deeper and more sensual meaning in the words of the Lord. Her sessions with Father Rick became increasingly passionate. Her newly discovered faith comforted and sustained her through the long months of loneliness and isolation. She dreamed about Father Rick at night and imagined herself as the minister's wife. What would it be like, making love to a minister? She imagined that he would be very gentle and loving.

Kyle

Kyle was becoming concerned about Aleecia's overtly religious text messages, thinking again how young and impressionable she was. She had told him about the choir director kicking her out and meeting three times a week with the associate minister for prayer sessions. Kyle was worried about what the church was filling her head with. Every time they texted, she'd sign off with "Jesus loves you." *What the fuck?* he wondered. He left his phone in his locker and ran onto the field.

"Hey, Kyle." He heard Julia's voice from inside the tunnel leading onto the field.

Julia was a freshman on the cheerleader squad. She was from Jacksonville.

Kyle stopped and turned around, slowly, for effect. "Yes, Ms. Julia?"

"I get excited watching you run down the field," she said.

Fuck, how come Aleecia never said things like that to him? She had never actually seen him play and she didn't seem at all interested in hearing about football.

"I hope I'm not distracting you from your duties," Kyle said. He turned and strode onto the field with a shit-eating grin on his face. He wasn't planning on making a move on Julia but he sure appreciated the attention.

///

The semester wound down.

Dwayne and me are coming home for Christmas, Kyle texted.

I'm playing Mary in the church pageant on the 23rd, Aleecia texted. Will u b here for that?

Sure, Kyle replied.

The church pageant? he wondered. He missed the old Aleecia and he didn't recognize this new person. Would she be parading around town on a donkey? Was she becoming delusional? If they kicked her out of the choir, why would they let her be in the Christmas pageant? He was afraid to ask.

Dwayne's last day of school was the nineteenth so Kyle packed up and drove to Fort Pierce on the twentieth. He wasn't sure what to expect when they pulled into Aleecia's driveway.

Aleecia was sitting on the porch in a wicker chair. When she stood up to greet them, Kyle was shocked to see how large she had become. She must have put on a hundred pounds. As Kyle approached her, she took his hands in hers and greeted him in a warm but platonic fashion.

"Hello," Aleecia said. "It is so wonderful to see you. And Dwayne! How are you?" Aleecia dropped Kyle's hands to reach out to Dwayne. "Welcome home."

"Is your mother here?" Kyle asked.

"No, she's working until seven," Aleecia said. "I made up the guesthouse for you. And dinner will be ready at six. Why don't y'all settle in?"

Kyle unloaded the car and carried the bags out back. The guesthouse was exactly the way he'd left it. *Imagine thinking that this would be our love nest*, he mused. It hadn't worked out that way. Was it his fault, for bringing Dwayne into the situation? Since he had left for school, clearly she had moved on. This homecoming was not going the way he had expected.

Aleecia appeared at the door. "I have dinner ready for Dwayne. Does he want to eat?" she asked.

"Yes!" Dwayne shouted and jumped up.

"He misses your cooking," Kyle said sheepishly. "Mostly we eat takeout."

"What about your cousin, Louise?" Aleecia asked. "Is that working out?"

"She watches him after school and when I have to travel to away games," Kyle said. "It's okay, she's nice to him."

"Oh right, your games," Aleecia said. "I heard you're having a great season. I guess you're like a star?"

"I don't like to brag," Kyle started.

"Yeah, me not so much," Aleecia interrupted. "They won't let me sing. And Mary doesn't even have a speaking part."

Kyle wasn't sure what to say. Was she trying to be funny?

"Let me feed Dwayne and then you can come help me set the table for mom, yes?" Aleecia said. "Okay then."

She wasn't really talking to Kyle; she seemed to be talking to herself. And she cradled her belly in a protective way. Kyle didn't recognize her. And not just because she had ballooned to three times the size she was when he last saw her. She seemed different in every way.

Twenty-four

KYLE

ALEECIA HAD MADE A BEEF STEW AND SALAD. KYLE helped her set the table and carry in the dishes.

"Hi, Ms. Rivera," Kyle said. "You're looking well."

"My, aren't we formal?" Aleecia's mom said.

"I'm sorry," Kyle whispered. "Aleecia seems different."

"Saint Aleecia," her mom said. "That's what we call her."

"Saint Aleecia?" Kyle asked.

"She's found Jesus," her mother said. "And

apparently we're witnessing the virgin birth, the Immaculate Conception."

"What the fuck?" Kyle asked.

"It's her way of coping," Aleecia's mom said. "I can't fault her. She's all alone here—the girls at school and in the choir have ostracized her. I remember going through that." She paused to take a sip of her wine cooler. "So how are you? I hear that you're the star running back."

"Things are good for me," Kyle said. "And Dwayne is doing okay. How can I help Aleecia?"

"Aleecia has found her own path, Kyle," Aleecia's mom said. "She's found peace. I'm not sure where this is going long-term, but let's try to be supportive. Can you do that?"

"Sure," Kyle said. "I got so caught up in my own world. I haven't really been in touch as much as I wanted. Is she mad at me?"

"No, sweetie," Aleecia's mom said. "She met this new minister and she seems happy. Let's just take it one day at a time."

"What should I be doing?" Kyle asked.

"I don't know," Aleecia's mom said. "Try a little harder to stay in touch with her? She seems to have lost touch with reality. We need to try to keep her grounded. Don't disappear on her the way her father did to me."

Kyle thought about it. He wanted to be there for Aleecia, but what if Aleecia no longer needed him to show up and be the father? *Maybe that is the right thing for her, but is it the right thing for my baby?*

Just then, Aleecia entered the room carrying a basket of bread. "Home-baked, y'all," Aleecia said.

"You've outdone yourself!" Aleecia's mother crowed.

Kyle concluded that the Rivera women found strength in abandonment. They were hoping he would exit the scene so Aleecia could prove herself to be the supermom that her mom had been. *Does she need to prove that she doesn't need me?* Kyle felt like he'd been shunted to the side—benched. He was angry with Aleecia's mom for not taking his side. He wasn't planning on running away. He wanted to stay and be a dad. He wasn't like the others. But he felt like he'd already been dismissed.

//

Kyle couldn't wait to get out of the house the next morning. Lucifer had texted that she wanted to see Dwayne.

Is Jared there? he texted.

Lucifer: He went to the Keys

//

Kyle dropped Dwayne off and met up with Steve.

"Aleecia has gotten weird, man," Kyle said.

"And fat!" Steve said. "She must weigh two hundred pounds."

"At least!" Kyle said. "What happened to her?"

"I don't know," Steve said. "We never see her any more. She doesn't hang out."

"I think her friends abandoned her," Kyle said. "Now, she spends all her time at church."

"Well, that's fucking weird," Steve said.

"That's what I'm saying," Kyle said. "I don't know how to talk to her. Even her mom calls her Saint Aleecia."

"What does this mean for you two?" Steve asked.

"I don't know," Kyle said. "She doesn't seem that interested in me. It's really uncomfortable staying at her house. Maybe I should just go back to Tallahassee. There's this hot cheerleader, Julia."

"Yeah?" Steve asked.

"She's really into me but we didn't do anything because of Aleecia," Kyle said. "But now, I don't think Aleecia even cares about me anymore."

"Well, whatever, you do," Steve said. "Don't knock her up."

"I don't think Julia would be that stupid," Kyle said and then immediately regretted it. "I'm not saying Aleecia is stupid. She used to be so smart and lively."

"And now she's a retarded water buffalo," Steve said.

Kyle punched Steve in the arm.

"Ow, man!" Steve cried. "I'm just sayin'."

//

Kyle swung by Lucifer's house and was furious to see Dwayne huddled on the front porch. He threw the gearshift into park and ran to the house.

"Dwayne, what's going on?"

"Mommy and Jared got into a fight," Dwayne said, sniffling.

"I thought Jared was in the Keys?" Kyle yelled.

"He came back," Dwayne said.

"Why didn't she text me?" Kyle asked.

"Jared broke her phone when she was trying to call 911," Kyle said. "Then they went to the hospital and told me to wait here for you."

"Hospital?' Kyle asked.

"Crystal got hurt bad," Dwayne said.

"Jared hurt Crystal?"

"She wouldn't stop crying and she pooped her pants and he hit her," Dwayne said. "Then she wouldn't wake up. When Mommy came home from Boyd's party, Crystal wouldn't wake up. That's when Mommy tried to call 911 and Jared broke her phone."

"Who is Boyd?" Kyle asked.

"I don't know," Dwayne said. "Jared said Mommy was fucking him for Oxy. What does that mean?"

"Oh shit!" Kyle said. "I gotta get you out of here." He thought for a minute. He really didn't want to spend another week at Aleecia's house. "How about if we just head back to Tallahassee? We can put up our own tree and have our own little Christmas—just you and me, what do you think?"

"And Cousin Louise?" Dwayne asked. He sounded excited.

"What about Cousin Louise?" Kyle asked. "Do you want to be with her family?"

"She said she had something for me under her tree," Dwayne said.

"I had no idea!" Kyle exclaimed. "That's great! What if we run by Big Lots and pick up some toys for her kids and we'll wrap them up and stuff them in a bag? And then I'll text her that we're coming by on Christmas Eve?"

"Just like Santa Claus!" Dwayne cried.

"Yes!" Kyle said. "This year, let's be Santa Claus!"

Twenty-five

KYLE

KYLE PULLED INTO ALEECIA'S DRIVEWAY.

"Stay here," Kyle said to Dwayne. "I'll grab our stuff and we'll go."

Aleecia was sitting on the sofa, knitting.

"What's that?" Kyle asked.

"Knitting," Aleecia said without looking up.

"Knitting?" Kyle asked.

"I'm making a blanket for the baby," Aleecia said. "Pink, 'cause I think it's a girl. They say when you gain weight all over it's a girl. With a boy, you only gain weight in your belly. With boys, you look like you've swallowed a basketball. With girls, you become a whale."

"So it must be a girl," Kyle said.

Aleecia chuckled.

"Honey, I think I need to take Dwayne home," Kyle said.

"Home?" Aleecia asked. She stopped knitting and looked at him quizzically.

"Crystal is in the hospital," Kyle said. "Jared hit her." He was hoping this painted a picture for her and created a smoke screen for him. She'd know it was best for them to leave town.

"Oh dear," Aleecia said. She dropped her knitting and struggled to her feet. "Shouldn't we go to the hospital?"

"Yes, but," Kyle said. "Look, I think I need to get Dwayne as far away as I can. I think I need to take him home." He caught himself. "I mean to Tallahassee. I should take him back."

"What about Crystal?" Aleecia asked.

Kyle took her hands in his. "I know that you could be such a powerful presence for her. Your influence would be so good for her. But my mom and Jared, they don't know you. It could get ugly, and that wouldn't help Crystal. I think the best thing we can do right now is to get Dwayne to a safe place. Don't you agree?"

Aleecia went into saint mode and smiled beatifically. "Yes, of course you're right. You are a wonderful brother. We are truly blessed."

Kyle wanted to grab her by the shoulders and shake her, but he felt so glad to be released. He slunk to the guesthouse and gathered all of their stuff and jammed it into the back seat of the car.

Kyle poked his head inside the screen door. "Merry Christmas, Aleecia. I'm sure you'll be an awesome Mary."

"Oh," Aleecia said. "You're going to miss my pageant?"

"I'm so sorry, sweetie," Kyle said. "But Dwayne . . . you know?"

"Of course," Aleecia said. "You're so good to us."

Us? Kyle thought. Was he being good to her? He didn't think so. This sainthood thing scared him.

///

They had been on the road for two hours. Kyle struggled to find a clear channel on the radio while Dwayne played games on Kyle's phone.

"Will you miss Aleecia?" Kyle said.

"Why?" Dwayne asked. "Aren't we coming back?"

"Maybe not," Kyle said.

"Okay," Dwayne said, absently.

Aleecia

When Father Rick asked Aleecia to play the part of Mary in the Christmas pageant, she was thrilled. Father Rick was to play Joseph, and Aleecia imagined there might be some intimate moments. She arrived early for rehearsals, excited to spend more time with him. But, Father Rick was also the pageant director, so he was mostly preoccupied with all the other actors. Even the sheep had more lines than Mary.

"When is Kyle coming?" Aleecia's mother asked one morning at breakfast.

"He'll be here on Saturday," Aleecia said. "He's bringing Dwayne with him."

Aleecia felt conflicted. Kyle had been the love of her life, the father of her child. Maybe it was because he'd been gone so long, but she wasn't able to summon the feelings of passion and longing that she'd once had for him. She knew she wanted him in her life, but she wasn't sure if she loved him, anymore.

"Mama, how do you know if you love somebody?" Aleecia asked.

"Are we talking about Father Rick?" her mother asked.

Aleecia's face was burning. "No!" she cried. "I meant Kyle. I just don't know how I feel about him anymore."

"You'll know when you see him," her mother said. "Listen to your heart."

Aleecia went into her room and logged onto Facebook.

Aleecia: I'm not sure I love Kyle anymore

Luciana: Is there someone else?

Shawna: He's been away all semester, right? Maybe you just need some 1-on-1 time

Aleecia: That's what my mom says. But I'm not sure I want to see him

Luciana: Like I said! Is there someone else?

Aleecia: I shouldn't be saying this

Isabella: There IS someone else!

Aleecia: Father Rick, my minister—well he's the assistant minister

Shawna: How old is he?

Aleecia: I don't know. 28, 29?

Jasmine: Is he hot?

Aleecia: Yesssss

Isabella: Watch out Kyle! You have competition

Aleecia: Maybe Kyle doesn't love me anymore?

Luciana: You'll find out soon enough—give us an update, girl!

///

Aleecia sat on the front porch in the wicker chair, anxiously rocking back and forth. She closed her eyes and prayed.

Dear God, please let me feel love for this man who is the father of my beloved child. Father Rick had repeatedly referred to her baby as her beloved child. It felt good when he said that.

When Kyle pulled into the driveway and stepped out of the car, she knew right away. She admired his animal grace, his handsome physique, and his flashing smile. But she knew she didn't love him the way she had come to love Jesus and Father Rick. A sense of peace washed over her. She was happy to welcome him into her home but she knew that she no longer wanted to be with him.

The next day, when Kyle announced he was taking Dwayne back to Tallahassee, Aleecia was so relieved. She wanted this to be the final goodbye, but she didn't have the courage to speak her mind. *Let's let some time pass and we'll see*, she thought.

Twenty-six

ALEECIA

AFTER THE VISIT IN DECEMBER, KYLE'S TEXTS ARRIVED less frequently. He sent an emoji kiss on New Year's Eve and an emoji rose on Valentine's Day, and then nothing.

Aleecia's due date came and went. Dr. Janec had warned her that her weight gain (she hated the word obesity) would create complications in labor and that she would most likely require a C-section. They scheduled the operation for April first: April Fools' Day. Aleecia took delight in that.

She texted Kyle: The baby is coming on April 1. Do

you want to be here? Without waiting for a response she texted the same message to Father Rick.

Father Rick responded immediately: Of course!

Aleecia regretted texting Kyle. What if he also wanted to be here, how would she handle that? She took comfort in the knowledge that Father Rick would handle the situation gracefully. And besides, she would be sedated the whole time.

It took a couple of days for Kyle to reply: Sorry babe, I can't miss class. Send pix!

That sealed it. In Aleecia's mind, Kyle was no longer the father of her child. She dreamed that Father Rick would marry her and adopt her daughter. Kyle would be forever in the rear-view mirror.

Aleecia's mother woke up at her usual hour on April first and then rolled over and nodded off, relieved that she didn't have to report to work today. They were supposed to be at the hospital at seven. At six, she knocked tentatively on Aleecia's door.

"Aleecia?" her mom whispered.

Aleecia moaned and rolled over.

"Aleecia?" her mom spoke a little louder. "We need to go."

"Go?" Aleecia sounded confused.

"To the hospital," her mom said. "Aleecia, wake up!"

//

Aleecia lay on a gurney in a hallway, wearing only a paper gown and cap, covered with a thin blanket, prepped for surgery. Nurses and interns whizzed by, gossiping and flirting. Aleecia became more and more anxious and she was shivering, not so much from cold but from sheer terror. Did these people know what they were doing?

Someone noticed the tears streaking down her face and wheeled her gurney into an operating suite.

Dr. Janec appeared at the foot of Aleecia's gurney. The deep circles under her eyes were magnified by her glasses. She looked weary and agitated. Aleecia was petrified by the idea of being sliced open by an angry, sleep-deprived doctor. She became convinced that she was going to die here in this room.

"Aleecia, what is the problem?" Dr. Janec demanded.

"I'm scared," Aleecia whispered.

An anesthesiologist intern spoke from behind Aleecia's head. "I could just put her under."

Aleecia cried out. "No!"

Dr. Janec glared at the intern. "No," she said.

"Aleecia," Dr. Janec said. "This baby needs to be born. Are you going to help us?"

"Yes," Aleecia whispered.

"Good girl," Dr. Janec said. "Now Dr. Leavitt is going to put you to sleep. When you wake up, your baby—do you have a name?"

"No," Aleecia mumbled. "Maybe Mia?"

"What did you say?" Dr. Janec asked. "Mia?"

"Yes, Mia," Aleecia said.

"It's time for Mia to be born," Dr. Janec said. "Now be a good girl and let Dr. Leavitt put you to sleep. When you wake up, Mia will be here. Will you stop crying now?"

Aleecia nodded, still weeping.

//

When Aleecia came to, she was in a hospital room, alone. The door was open and she could see nurses walking in the hallway.

"Hello?" Aleecia called out.

A nurse appeared in the doorway. "Are we awake, Mommy?" the nurse asked. "Would you like me to bring Mia in? Your parents would like to come in as well."

"My parents?" For a second Aleecia thought that the father she never knew had come to meet his grandchild. Then she heard Father Rick's voice in the hallway.

"You came!" Aleecia cried as Father Rick entered the room.

"How are you feeling?" Aleecia's mom asked.

Aleecia tried to sit up and then yelped in pain.

The nurse rushed in, holding Mia. "I told you not to move. You call me first," the nurse said. "Here, Ms. Rivera, why don't you sit in the chair and hold Mia?" Aleecia's mom sat down on the recliner, and the nurse gingerly handed her the baby. Aleecia's mom made cooing noises and breathed in the baby's scent.

"Now Aleecia," the nurse said. "You just relax and I'll adjust the bed. Your incision is going to be quite tender for several weeks."

Father Rick approached the bed and took Aleecia's hand in his.

"Have you been here long?" Aleecia asked.

"I came when your mom texted me," Father Rick said. "We sat together in the waiting room. It didn't take long—maybe an hour."

"Can I hold my baby?" Aleecia asked.

"Not until the sedation has worn off," the nurse said. "I'll check on you in a bit."

"Can I hold her?" Father Rick asked. He took Mia

from Aleecia's mom and carried her to Aleecia's bed. He leaned in close and said, "Look at this beautiful little soul."

Aleecia was overcome. She had never been this close to Father Rick before. She could feel his warm breath and smell his sweet musk. And the way he tenderly held Mia, she just knew that he loved her and that he would be there for her and Mia, forever.